'And now, get out of my life,' Ric Burnett had told Glenna, firmly and cruelly—and she had had no choice but to go. That was eight years ago, but now, in New Zealand, they had met again. But Ric was a married man, and she had quite got over him anyway. Or had she?

Books you will enjoy
by DAPHNE CLAIR

DARLING DECEIVER

At seventeen, Carissa had been a silly, romantic teenager in love with a dream called Cade Fernand—which was why she had behaved the way she had on the one occasion they had met. Now, eight years later, they had met again, and she had no reason to suppose Cade remembered anything about her. But he still remembered—and still despised her. And Carissa realised, hopelessly, that her feelings for him had not changed either . . .

SOMETHING LESS THAN LOVE

Just what had gone wrong with Vanessa's marriage? True, her husband Thad had been badly injured in a car crash soon after the wedding, but he was recovering now. It wasn't that—it was his curious, bitter, suspicious attitude to her. What was she supposed to have *done*?

THE JASMINE BRIDE

Rachel didn't think it mattered in the least that she was so much younger than Damon Curtis—at any rate, it hadn't stopped him marrying her. But she was also very much more inexperienced; wasn't that going to be the rock on which the marriage would founder before it had even begun?

THE SLEEPING FIRE

Adam Broome—the 'new Broome' as he soon became to all the staff of *Lively Lady* magazine—was living up to his name and introducing all kinds of changes, and editor Lee Palmer wasn't sure she was happy about them. She felt happier about Adam himself, who was undeniably attractive. But then she wasn't the only one to feel that way about him, was she . . . ?

A STREAK
OF GOLD

BY

DAPHNE CLAIR

MILLS & BOON LIMITED
17-19 FOLEY STREET
LONDON W1A 1DR

First published 1978
Australian copyright 1980
Philippine copyright 1980
This edition 1980

© Daphne Clair 1978

ISBN 0 263 73255 X

Set in Linotype Baskerville 10 on 11½ pt.

Made and printed in Great Britain by
Richard Clay (The Chaucer Press), Ltd., Bungay, Suffolk

CHAPTER ONE

THE calm sea had turned to a sheet of silver, reflecting the clouded sky. Across the Firth of Thames, named by some nostalgic explorer after another body of water on the other side of the world, the land mass was almost obscured by mist.

The girl sitting under one of the massive pohutu-kawa trees that lined the Coromandel peninsula of New Zealand shivered as she realised that the warmth of the day was gone. There had been clouds before, scudding lightly across the blue sky, but now they had covered it completely, and the gently lapping water no longer looked friendly and inviting as it had earlier in the afternoon, when she had taken a swim. It was cold and depressing, and Glenna Lawrence began to slip back into the mood from which she had been trying to escape when she decided to take her red Mini car and drive to one of the secluded bays on the coast, for a swim and sunbathe.

There was no question of sunbathing now, she told herself wryly, as she huddled into her towelling poncho and began under its cover to pull on her crumpled jeans over the still-damp swimsuit.

If only this particular date had fallen on a weekday, she would have been kept far too busy to brood. Her work, teaching at a special school for physically handi-capped children, was demanding enough to require all her resources when she was in the classroom, and a

5

good deal of her time and energy when she was out of
it.

But yesterday, Saturday, she had got her head down
and prepared her lesson plans for the whole of the coming week, and having attended the service held in the
chapel that morning, had found herself at a loose end
and without company for the rest of the day. The other
teacher who helped her with the forty-five lively young-
sters who lived at the Helen Duke Memorial School
lived with her parents in the township of Thames itself,
and had an attentive boy-friend. And the nursing staff,
of course, had rostered weekends. Glenna had two good
friends among the nurses, Peggy Watson and Cleo
Brent, but neither had been free to accompany her
today.

She would not have been very good company for
them, anyway, she thought, sighing as she picked up
her towel and sandals and made her way towards her
car, avoiding the smooth grey stones that littered the
sand.

She should not have come to a beach, she told herself
irritably. She should have known it would be bound to
bring back memories . . .

She met him on a beach in France. She had been watching him, at first thinking idly what a good-looking man
he was, and she supposed every girl's idea of the typical
Frenchman. Tall, dark and handsome didn't even be-
gin to describe the lithe attraction of his rather scantily
clad body with its deep tan, and his crisp-looking dark
hair crowning an almost perfectly male profile.

Glenna watched him look around the beach, which
was a popular tourist one, and fairly crowded, and then
he walked towards the water, casually dropping his
towel quite close to a lusciously curvy girl who was
sunning herself in a very daring striped bikini. He

didn't look at or speak to her, but Glenna was sure he knew quite well that the girl had raised herself on one elbow and was watching him enter the water.

He swam for about twenty minutes, and he was good in the water. Glenna, without watching him all the time, found her eyes sufficiently drawn to him to notice that. When he came out, the striped bikini was lying motionless as though its owner had never noticed her handsome neighbour, and Glenna grinned to herself as he picked up the towel, flicking sand over the girl, so that she wriggled and sat up.

The man's lips moved, and he stooped towards the girl. Apologising, Glenna thought. And a very smart move, too. He had dropped down on the sand now, close to the bikini-clad girl, and was talking in earnest. Chatting her up, obviously. How long, Glenna wondered, before he persuaded the girl to have a drink with him, or go for a walk, or perhaps accept a dinner invitation? She didn't, from this distance, anyway, look the type to be able to resist his looks and charm for long. And turning on the charm he certainly was. He was leaning close and smiling at her now, and his smile was something, it really was.

Glenna, at nineteen, had three brothers and a sister near her own age, the others ranging from eighteen— her 'little brother' as she teasingly called Tony, deriding his six feet of young manhood, to Robin's twenty-three. Alison, the other girl, was the twin of Peter, a beauty whose experience of the 'lines' she had handed to her by hopeful young men she passed on with some sisterly advice to the younger Glenna. Robin and Peter, too, were protective of her, and made sure that she knew what unscrupulous methods some of their contemporaries were capable of using to get a girl to do what they wanted.

Glenna had been out with men, had been kissed several times, but when things got intense, she had a way of turning them off with a laughing comment that let them know she was flattered, but not interested in more than friendship.

Some took off sulkily for greener pastures, but she found that she never lacked for an escort. Some men appreciated friendship, and liked her for her no-nonsense attitude and her pleasant and occasionally stringent conversation.

This Frenchman, she was thinking, was exactly the type her family had warned her of. What they hadn't realised was that few men of this type would look her way. She was pleasant enough to look at, with her dark grey eyes and shoulder-length dark-blonde hair, a nice nose and a pretty mouth that could sometimes firm into unexpected stubbornness, but she was by no means the 'gorgeous looker' that even their brothers admitted Alison was.

Like that lovely French girl, who was laughing at something the man had said, throwing back a mane of dark hair and giving him, no doubt, a fine view of her throat and the splendid lines of her body ...

But the girl had suddenly stopped laughing, and was sitting up, looking up into the face of a blond young giant of a man who was standing and glowering at the two on the sand.

She spoke, waving a casual hand at the dark man beside her, who stood up and offered his hand to the other.

After a moment, the newcomer took the hand and nodded briefly, making some short comment. He was enormous, and topped the dark man, who was no midget by any standards, by a couple of inches.

He sat down and possessively put his arm around the girl, and the other man picked up his towel, nodded briefly, and straightened.

For an instant he looked straight into Glenna's eyes, and she received a shock of surprise. Her face must have been full of inward laughter, for she was thinking that he had decided discretion was the better part of valour, and the unexpected development in the little drama she had been watching struck her as inexpressibly funny.

Hoping he had not realised she had been watching, she hastily averted her eyes and made a great play of studying a family group which included a small girl wearing an absurdly frilly playsuit, and a slightly larger boy, who were tussling over a bucket which they both wanted.

She knew very well that the dark man was walking in her direction, but told herself that he would no doubt pass straight by her. Only when a pair of brown feet and straight brown legs, fuzzed with dark hair and still slightly damp, stopped right within her vision, did she finally look up. It seemed a long way to his face.

He was even better looking at close quarters, and his eyes were dark, somewhere between hazel and brown. The smouldering light in them matched the slight grimness that just now hung about his mouth.

He addressed her in French, and although it was not strictly true, she replied quickly, 'I'm sorry, *monsieur*, I don't speak French,' and looked away as though she was not interested in trying.

'Okay, we'll speak English, then,' he said easily, without a trace of an accent, and she was so surprised she turned to look at him again.

'You're English?'

'Yes. Surprised? The place is full of tourists, you know. There are probably more foreigners than French people on this beach. Like our Scandinavian friend, over there.' He nodded towards where the blond giant was nuzzling the bikini girl's ear.

'Is that what he is?'

'Yes—big, isn't he?' he asked cheerfully. His towel plopped down on the sand damply, and without asking for permission, he sat down beside Glenna. 'Do you blame me for retreating?'

Her mouth twitched at the corner, and she bit her lip.

'It's all right,' he said resignedly. The hint of temper with which he had accosted her seemed to have vanished. 'You can laugh. I guess it must have looked pretty funny from here.'

She did laugh, then, lying back on her towel, and he propped himself up on one elbow and grinned down at her.

'*That* funny?' he asked ruefully, raising an eyebrow.

She smiled up at him, liking the way he could laugh at himself. 'I thought you were French. I was admiring your technique——'

'Oh?' A speculative gleam replaced some of the humour in his eyes.

'Oh, no, you don't!' she said, sitting up and away from him. 'I'm only a spectator.'

'Scared?' he jeered.

'No, just cautious.'

'At your age?'

'You don't know my age.'

'Eighteen? Twenty?'

'Nineteen.'

'Have you a name?'

'Yes, but I don't usually give it to strange men.'

He laughed. 'You *are* cautious. What's in a name? Mine's Alaric Burnett. My friends usually call me Ric.'

'Glenna Lawrence,' she said resolutely, after a pause.

'Pretty,' he commented, eyeing her with a look that said, *you are too.*

She cast him a derisive look, and he frowned. 'What was that for?'

'What was what for?'

'You know. The way you looked at me.'

'Just that that technique of yours is a bit obvious,' she said dryly.

For a moment he looked almost sulky. It was all she could do not to laugh at him again, but she knew this time he would not be so complacent. It wouldn't have done him any harm, but the sulky look made him look like a small boy, and suddenly she couldn't hurt him.

'You know, you're quite good-looking,' she said kindly. 'You don't need to hand out a line.'

Sheer astonishment crossed his handsome features, to be followed by a shout of laughter.

Glenna flushed, feeling distinctly foolish. Just because for a moment he had looked like one of the children she intended to teach when she was fully qualified, she had treated him like one. No wonder he was laughing at her! She started to rise and gather up her towel and beach bag.

'Where are you going?' he asked.

'Back to my hotel.'

'Let me take you,' he offered, standing too. 'It will only take me a minute to change.'

'No, thanks. It was nice talking to you,' she said politely. 'Goodbye, Mr Burnett.'

'Hold on,' he said, catching her arm in a strong grip. 'Have dinner with me tonight?'

She shook her head firmly. 'I have a dinner date, thank you.' She didn't tell him she intended to eat at her hotel with the girl friend who was sharing this holiday.

'Tomorrow?'

Tentatively, she wriggled her arm and he set it free. 'I—don't think so.'

'Look, I'm perfectly respectable,' he said.

'I'm sure you are, but——'

'But you don't like me.'

He fleetingly resumed the sulky look, and she said exasperatedly, 'Of course I like you! I mean—how can I know, when I've only just met you?'

'And how will you know if you don't see me again? Dinner tomorrow night, okay?'

Now he looked pleading, and somehow she found herself agreeing.

Back at her hotel, she mentally castigated herself for being taken in by a practised wolf. Probably that sulky little boy look was deliberately put on, she told herself. He had obviously been looking for a pick-up on the beach, and when the Scandinavian giant had frightened him off his first choice, he had looked around and decided to take second best. Probably he had picked on her because she didn't look glamorous enough to have a giant of her own in tow, she reflected gloomily.

Jane, her friend, was delighted that Glenna had a date. She herself had become friendly with a nice, lively French boy, and although the two of them included Glenna and sometimes the boy brought along a friend to make a foursome, Glenna knew that sometimes they would like to be alone. That was why she had been on the beach this afternoon, pleading that she was too tired after a night out the night before to go on a sightseeing tour with them.

She dressed carefully for her dinner date, discarding one outfit after another, and finally settling for a deep blue sleeveless dress that she had owned for a long time. It always felt comfortable and looked right for any occasion.

'You look lovely,' Alaric Burnett said, when he called for her. Glenna thanked him coolly, still smarting under the idea that she was second best, and wondering how she compared to the girl on the beach for looks.

The sidelong looks that some of the girls gave him at the small restaurant to which he took her only made her more restive, and her replies to his conversational efforts were polite and distant.

She hardly noticed that the food was delicious, cooked to perfection as only the French could do it, and when they got to the coffee stage, she didn't realise that he had given up trying to talk to her and was just looking at her as she absentmindedly stirred sugar into her cup.

'What's the matter?' he asked.

'Nothing's the matter,' she said, astonished. 'It's been a very nice meal, thank you. I've enjoyed it.'

'But you don't enjoy my company, is that it?'

'Whatever makes you think that? I'm having a very nice time.'

'*Nice!* Must you be so polite?'

'Must *you* be so rude?' she countered. 'I don't know about you, but *I* was brought up to be polite.'

'I apologise,' he muttered. 'It's just that I wanted to give you a good time, and it seems to me that you're not really enjoying this at all.'

'I'm sorry,' she said frigidly. 'I suppose your pick-ups are usually more appreciative of their good fortune.'

The silence was so intense that after a moment she had to look up. Her heart skipped a beat, because she realised he was furious. His mouth was tight and his eyes angry.

'I'm sorry,' she said again, genuinely meaning it this time. 'That was unforgivably rude of me.'

It took a few moments, but his features relaxed, and he put a warm hand over hers, saying, 'Not *unforgivably*, Glenna. But what suddenly happened to your so polite upbringing, hmm?'

She flushed, and he laughed.

'I don't look on you as a *pick-up*, Glenna,' he said seriously a few moments later. 'I went to the beach yesterday simply to swim. That girl caught my eye, and I thought it might be nice to get acquainted. I'm here on my own, and the prospect of having a nice French girl to show me round was pleasant. Well, it didn't work out quite as planned, but I'm very glad I happened to find *you*.'

She looked up and gave him a tentative smile. 'Aren't you disappointed I'm not French?'

'Are you disappointed that I'm not?'

She shook her head.

'I'm just glad you're you,' he said. 'And I want to get to know you a whole lot better. I have ever since I saw you laughing at me on the beach yesterday.'

If she was honest with herself, she wanted to know him a lot better, too.

She had only three weeks' holiday, and they spent as many hours of it together as they could, sightseeing, swimming, dining and dancing, sometimes with Jane and her French friend, sometimes alone.

She told him about her home in a small industrial town, and about her family—her three brothers and sister, and her lawyer father, and the mother who held her close-knit family together in the hollow of her hand.

'What about your family?' she asked.

'Both my parents died when I was young,' he said.

'Oh! How awful for you.'

'Not to worry,' he grinned. 'If you're picturing me as some poor little orphan, don't. I was too young to remember them. I wasn't shot into a children's home or anything dire like that. My uncle, my father's brother, took me in and made sure I was well cared for. When I was old enough, I went to boarding school—a good one. My uncle has literally been like a father to me. I don't believe I've ever really missed not having the real thing.'

'What do you do for a living?' she asked.

'I work with my uncle.'

'Doing what?'

'Oh—complicated, my sweet. Glorified office boy, that's me,' he grimaced. 'The firm is one of those that has a finger in practically every pie.'

'Oh, high finance and all that?'

'Very much so, especially "all that".'

'Do you like it?'

'Not especially,' he said slowly. 'But I don't want to let my uncle down.'

'Oh,' she said wisely. 'You mean he wants you to carry on the family firm, or something?'

'Something like that. He has no children of his own.'

'That's emotional blackmail, you know,' she said seriously.

'No, *no!*' he protested. 'There's nothing like that. If there was anything I particularly wanted to do, he'd tell me to go and do it with his blessing, believe me. I have no particular desire to do anything else. So I might just as well stay as I am, and keep everyone happy.'

'I've always known what I wanted to do.'

'Teaching?'

'Yes, I used to line up my dolls and play school by the hour, as a child.'

'I can imagine it.' His smile crinkled the corners of his eyes. 'I'll bet you always had that teacher's manner. I noticed it the very first time I met you.'

'What teacher's manner?' she demanded indignantly. She imagined him seeing her as a stereotyped school-marm, all starchy and stern.

'A sort of kindly firmness,' he told her. 'Just the

thing for putting naughty little boys in their place.'

'Don't talk such nonsense,' she said firmly, and then blushed in confusion as he shouted with laughter.

'You see?' he said. 'No wonder I haven't dared to kiss you yet.'

At which she blushed more hotly than ever, turning away so that he shouldn't see it. She had wondered that he hadn't attempted to kiss her. She knew very well that he wanted to, and he wasn't the type to let the grass grow under his feet, of that she was very sure. They had known each other for two weeks, and in another week she would be going home.

'Never mind,' he said in her ear. 'I intend to, one of these days.'

'Don't be silly!' she said crossly.

'All right, teacher,' he answered, so meekly that she longed to turn around and hit him, but she could imagine what he would make of *that*, and didn't dare.

She knew she was falling in love with him. And for that reason she both hoped and feared that he would, eventually, kiss her.

Because this was the classic 'holiday romance', she supposed. The short, sweet affair that could never last. It was, for her, the first time, and she wanted to loiter in the shallows before plunging into unknown deeps of passion. She wasn't sure that she could cope with passion. And yet she was well aware that time was short, her holiday drawing to a close. Would he keep in touch afterwards, or did he look on this as just a pleasant interlude, to be forgotten once he was back home, working in his uncle's office in London?

She decided to take each day as it came, and refuse to think of tomorrow.

Afterwards, she thought the nicest thing about that first kiss, when it did occur, was that it just happened.

She knew that Ric had no more expected it just there and then than she had.

They had been dancing, and were walking back to her hotel, a little crazy with wine and the scented night, the sound of the sea not so far away, and their delight in each other. The street was deserted, and she danced a few steps ahead of him, humming the last tune they had danced to, and bumped into a lamp-post.

'Pardon, *monsieur*,' she said, backing off and giving the lamp-post a grave curtsy.

Someone down the street opened a window, and the strains of a waltz tune, from a radio or record, drifted softly into the street.

Glenna rose from her curtsy and crooked her arm around the lamp-post and danced around it in waltz time.

Ric's soft laughter rose behind her, and he spun her into his arms. 'If you want to dance, dance with me, not a lamp-post!' He held her close and they twirled down the street, their feet seeming to float as if by magic on the rough surface, until at last she stumbled and he caught her close to stop her falling.

They were under another lamp, and as she looked up, laughing and breathless, it made a nimbus round his dark head, and she couldn't see his face at all. But she heard his breath as he spoke her name, and her heart gave a tiny thud before he bent his head and kissed her.

It was very gentle and slow, and at first his lips barely skimmed hers, but as her hands moved up and over his shoulders, to meet behind his neck, his lips firmed and parted hers, and his arms gathered her closer to his warm body.

He released her slowly, too. And as she felt cold air between them, she kept her eyes closed, and rested her head on his shoulder as he turned her with his arm, to walk by his side.

Reluctantly she opened her eyes, and saw that they had nearly reached the hotel. His arm was firmly around her waist, and they walked in silence until they reached the lighted doorway.

He turned her to face him, and she looked up into his eyes, with all her heart in hers.

'Oh, sweet!' he said unsteadily, and pulled her close. 'Will I see you tomorrow?'

'Yes,' she whispered.

'First thing in the morning, I'll be here,' he promised. He pressed a kiss on her cheek, and then his fingers turned her face up, and he kissed her lips, briefly and a little fiercely. 'Tomorrow,' he said, and gave her a little push towards the door.

CHAPTER TWO

DRIVING slowly on the twisting seaside road which led back to the school, Glenna found her eyes filled with tears. Impatiently, she brushed them away, and tried resolutely to think of other things. It was all in the past, she told herself, and there was no point in making herself miserable over it again, now.

She turned off the highway before it passed through Thames, and followed the winding road that led to the school. It was a converted homestead, eighty years old but well preserved. Built of heart kauri, probably the hardest wood in the world, she had been told, it could be expected to stand for another eighty years, at least.

The grounds were beautifully kept in order by a full-time gardener who lived in a cottage a little way from the main house, and another building, of tapestry brick, modern but carefully designed to complement the main building, consisted of staff quarters, mainly small self-contained flats. There was also a communal staff dining room, and a lounge where they could fore-gather if they wished.

Glenna drove up the poplar-lined drive and parked her car in the space provided behind her flatlet. After making herself a meal she went to the lounge, hoping for company. The few there were absorbed in a drama showing on the colour TV set, but she found it not gripping enough to keep her thoughts at bay.

Eventually the story came to an end, and someone turned to her and said, 'Well! That was something different, anyway. What did you think of it, Glenna?'

'They all seemed to be getting frightfully intense over nothing very much, didn't they?' she said absently.

Another girl laughed. 'That's our sensible Glenna!' she said, not unkindly. 'I'm sure you never get yourself all worked up about nothing—as I'm afraid *I* sometimes do!'

More friendly laughter greeted this, which Glenna joined in. 'Well, there's not much point, is there, if things can be sorted out in a few minutes, just by everyone keeping calm and thinking straight?'

'Well, if everyone had done that in the TV story, there would have *been* no story, would there? And wouldn't life be boring if we never got intense about things?'

It might be boring, Glenna thought later, as she prepared for bed, but she wouldn't have minded that, if it had been less painful. She wondered what the others would say, if they knew that their so sensible Glenna was getting herself all worked up today, about a love affair that went wrong eight years ago.

She remembered how happy she had felt when Ric announced that he had changed the date of his departure for home to coincide with hers. He had not been able to get on the same flight, but had made her promise to wait for him at the airport, and let him take her and Jane out to dinner, before they went to the hotel where they had booked to stay the night before travelling to their hometown.

They had not talked of the future, and he watched her face with a hint of anxiety when he told her of his changed plans. She had no thought of hiding her delight, for surely it was a sign that he wanted to keep seeing her, that their romance was more than just a holiday one?

They were in a secluded little bay which they had found, picnicking on grass just a little way above the sand. She was so delighted that she leaned over and kissed him quite naturally on the mouth. He was not expecting it, and was caught off balance, pulling her with him as he fell back on the soft grass.

She giggled and kissed him again, and he rolled over, pinning her beneath his body, and began kissing her in earnest, with little of his usual gentleness.

At first she lay quiescent in his hold. Then she became a little frightened, and began to struggle.

Ric let her go, and sat up, his back rigid.

For a moment Glenna lay there, feeling slightly dizzy, then she too, sat up, wrapping her arms around her knees and resting her head on them, so that her hair fell over her face.

She felt his hand, gentle on the back of her neck. He pushed aside her hair and dropped a featherlight kiss on her sun-warm skin. 'Sorry, sweet,' he said gently. 'I scared you, didn't I?'

'It was my fault,' she mumbled, into her arm. 'I didn't mean to tease.'

'You weren't teasing,' he said. 'You were just being your own sweet self. I forgot that you're only a baby.'

Her head jerked up at that, her eyes wide with angry hurt.

'I'm not a baby! I'm nineteen, and I've been kissed before!'

'*Yes?*' he said, and she looked at the sudden warning light in his dark eyes defiantly. 'I'm twenty-six, and I've kissed a few girls in my time, too. And some of them were a hell of a lot more experienced than you!'

She felt as though he had hit her. 'I'm sorry if I disappoint you!' she said stiffly, and got to her feet. Distractedly, she looked about for her things, but he was standing, too. He put an arm about her and pulled her closer, ignoring the stiffening of her body against him.

'Glenna, don't!' he said on a laughing moan. 'I'm trying to tell you I—I've enjoyed your kisses more than any other girl's.'

'It's very kind of you to say so,' she said politely, because of course he couldn't mean it. He was trying to be nice because he had hurt her feelings.

'*Glenna!*' His voice was full of exasperation as his hands gripped her arms and held her a little away from him. 'You don't believe me, do you?' For an instant, the sulky boy look that she had seen the first day was on his face. Then he smiled a little wryly, and said, 'I guess that may be just as well.'

He didn't kiss her when he left her at her hotel, and she lay awake that night wondering why. But the next day he was the same as ever, and happiness thrust the memory of the small quarrel to the back of her mind.

The last day of their holiday, he asked for her home address, and wrote it into a small diary he pulled from his pocket.

'May I have yours?' she asked.

He hesitated, and she was suddenly frightened. Then he smiled. 'You're not afraid I won't contact you, are you?'

'No. And you needn't worry. I wouldn't——'

Chase him, she meant. Make a nuisance of herself. If he changed his mind about keeping in touch, she had no intention of embarrassing him.

'Stop it, Glenna!' he said roughly, as though reading her thoughts. 'Here——' he scribbled on a page of the diary and pulled it out and gave it to her. 'There's no need, that's all. Because I have every intention of seeing you again. And again, and again, and again.'

They waited for him at the airport, as planned, and when he saw Glenna he walked straight up and kissed her as though he hadn't seen her for weeks. And also as though he had every right. She let herself imagine that they were engaged, or even married, and Ric had been away and was now coming home—to her. Her daydreams gave her an air of sweet abstraction. He noticed it and pinched her cheek, saying, 'Hey! Where have you gone?'

She made a face at him, and turned away to collect her luggage.

Jane was diffident about dining with them, but they both insisted. She had shed a few tears at parting from her French boy-friend, with many promises to write, and Glenna was determined not to leave her alone to mope.

They dined in a small restaurant which specialised in all types of Eastern food. Ric was known there, and he chose the menu at their bidding, because both girls felt they wanted to try something exotic, but had no idea what the weird names on the menu card meant.

The main course was a veal dish, the meat simmered in a delicious spicy sauce. After that, Ric suggested a fruit dessert of apricots and whipped cream topped with a sprinkling of nutmeg.

'Delicious!' Jane leaned back with a sigh of content and lit a cigarette. 'Thank you, Ric.'

'Glad you enjoyed it,' he smiled. 'Coffee?'

'Not for me, thanks. I'll just go and put on some lipstick, if you two will excuse me for a while.'

She rose and went to the discreetly marked door in a corner of the room.

'She's being tactful,' Ric remarked, smiling at Glenna across the table.

'Yes. And now I can't think of a thing to say!'

He grinned. 'Coffee for you? You can have Turkish if you like.'

'Is that good?'

'I think so.'

'Then yes, thank you.'

Ric ordered it, and Glenna's eyes wandered round the restaurant, catching the eye of a solemn boy of about six at an adjoining table, apparently dining with his parents. He had very wide dark eyes, and was holding his knife and fork with great care, as though he was not used to dining out. She supposed this must be some special occasion, and she smiled at him.

Ric lifted his brows, said, 'Someone you know?' And turned to see who was attracting her attention.

'No,' she said. 'Just the little boy at the next table.'

After a surprised little stare, the boy smiled back with a hint of mischief, and as Ric returned his gaze to Glenna, she laughed and said, 'I think he's a nice little boy.'

'As long as you're only looking at *little* boys.'

'You remind me of one, sometimes.'

'I *what*?' His amazement was so patent that she laughed again.

'I've sometimes wondered if you did it on purpose.'

Now he looked thoroughly disgusted, saying forcefully, 'If you still think that I've been spinning some line to you——'

The waiter brought their coffee, and Glenna quickly changed the subject as Jane rejoined them.

As they left the restaurant, there seemed to be quite a crowd of people on the pavement outside, and as a fire engine wailed by, they realised why. A little way down the street a building was alight, fire licking at its windows from the inside, and even as they stared one of the windows shattered and the fire began leaping up the outside wall. The fire engine had stopped and the firemen were leaping from it and busily unloading hoses and equipment.

An excited exclamation made Glenna turn to see the

boy from the other table emerging from the restaurant with his parents. No doubt the thrill of seeing a fire engine in action would set the seal on his evening out, she thought as she watched him lead his reluctant parents towards the scene of the action.

'I'm afraid there's no chance of getting a taxi from here just now,' Ric told the two girls. 'I take it you don't want to stay and watch the excitement?'

They both disclaimed any desire to do so, knowing that crowds of onlookers could only hinder the firemen in their task.

'Right. Well, let's start moving before the crowd gets any worse. We'd better go that way, I'm afraid,' he added, indicating the direction in which the burning building lay. 'The main road is there, so come on while we can still get through easily.'

As they began to walk, edging through the rapidly increasing numbers of people on the opposite side of the road from the fire, another fire engine came noisily into the street, followed by a police car. The crowd suddenly surged forward, and the policemen got out of their car and started to urge people back. Ric and the two girls had been carried willy-nilly to the edge of the crowd, and Glenna heard a male voice shout something about 'oxygen cylinders' and 'risk of explosion'. The voices of the policemen seemed to grow more urgent, and she looked up to see that the burning building was some sort of factory. She saw something else too, and wrenched her hand from Ric's firm hold to turn and confirm that the small figure standing alone and far too close to the building, behind the policemen and hidden from the firemen by the bulk of one of the fire engines, was indeed her little unknown friend from the restaurant.

Someone yelled 'Look out!' And some of the firemen began to run back from the fire. The small figure stood riveted, and Ric gave Glenna a hard shove back into the crowd behind her and began running the other way as there was a deafening roar and a part of the wall near the door of the blazing factory seemed to disintegrate, pieces flying outwards into the street. A sheet of flame billowed out before Glenna's horrified eyes as she regained her balance, and the two figures silhouetted against fire seemed to have disappeared.

She heard herself screaming Ric's name as the crowd surged around her with shocked murmurs and cries, and when she fought her desperate way through with a ruthlessness that was utterly foreign to her, there was a bunch of firemen and policemen bent over, blocking her view, and then quickly carrying two still figures away through the shocked crowd.

She saw the boy's mother and father, faces ghastly and stunned, accost one of the policemen and get hustled in front of him. And then Jane took her arm and they too followed.

The ambulances were quite quick, but there was a nightmare of explaining to be done before she was allowed to accompany a blanket-swathed Ric in one of them, and at the hospital they whisked him quickly away while she answered more questions.

She gave them his uncle's address and the address Ric had given her, but it seemed that they had trouble contacting the uncle, because they came and asked her more questions about relatives, and she couldn't help.

'We're not relatives,' Jane explained. 'We were just out for the evening with Mr Burnett.'

Then it was suggested that they might like to go home. There was nothing they could do, the nurse said kindly. They might like to ring in the morning.

'No!' said Glenna. 'Can you tell me how bad it is?'

'We don't know ourselves, yet, I'm afraid. He's been taken to theatre, and it may be some hours. Wouldn't you be better to go and have some rest?'

Glenna looked at the nurse wonderingly. How on earth did this woman imagine she could *rest* when Ric might be dying? she thought.

She stayed, and they promised to bring her news as soon as it was possible. Jane stayed too, silently sympathetic and occasionally offering hopeful words of comfort. She even procured a cup of tea from somewhere, and Glenna sipped it gratefully and began to think again.

'The little boy,' she said. 'Do you know how he is, Jane?'

'One of the nurses said he's going to be all right. He was knocked out, and he has an injured foot. But he's in no danger. *Kids!*' she added with exasperation. 'Why did the silly little twit have to go so near? He's old enough to know better.'

'He was fascinated by the fire engine. I suppose he didn't think. He's quite little.'

'You're a sucker for kids, Glenna.'

Glenna even managed a smile. 'Perhaps.'

'It was a couple of metal cylinders that exploded,' Jane said. 'No one else was badly hurt. The firemen and police were wearing helmets, of course.'

She went on chattering, but Glenna only half-heard. She was grateful for the company, and even for Jane's efforts at conversation, but her mind was concentrated on one thing— Ric.

It was hours later before a Sister came down the corridor to the small waiting room. Glenna stood up to face her as she came in.

'You're waiting for news of Mr Burnett?' she asked briskly, looking from Glenna to Jane.

'Yes. Is he going to be all right?' Glenna asked.

'He won't die,' the woman said cheerfully. 'He's really a lucky man. But he may have to be in hospital

for some time, I'm afraid. He has only superficial
burns, but quite a few pieces of metal managed to find
their way into him, and it took some time to remove
them. He isn't going to be very comfortable for a while.
Now, are you Mr Burnett's fiancée?'

'No. I'm—we're friends.' Glenna wished she could
claim some closer relationship. 'Have you contacted his
uncle?'

'Yes. He has apparently been out of town on a business trip, but he's returning now, and will be seeing his
nephew later today.'

'Oh. May I——'

'He can't have visitors just yet. And in any case he's
still sleeping off the anaesthetic. I suggest you come
back later today, and perhaps talk with Mr Burnett's
uncle. I'm sure you need some rest.'

At the hotel, before she slept, Glenna whispered to
herself, 'He's alive. He's alive and will be all right!'

Ric's uncle was a surprise. He was tall and broad, and
looked a good deal younger than his age, which she
knew to be forty-seven. His hair was brown, with a
slight grizzled look about the neat sideburns, and his
eyes were very much the colour of his nephew's.

'Miss Lawrence,' he greeted her, putting out his
hand, and enfolding hers in a firm grip. 'They tell me
you were with Ric when this thing happened.'

'Yes, we had dinner together, with another friend of
mine. Have you seen him?'

'Yes. He wasn't conscious, but I sat with him a while.'

They were standing in a little waiting room. When
Glenna entered the ward and asked for permission to
see Ric, she had been told his uncle was here, and asked
to speak to him first.

'How is he?' she asked.

'As well as can be expected,' he said harshly, 'as they
will tell you.' She understood his anxiety.

'I'd like to see him,' she said.

'Miss Lawrence, is your name Glenna?'

'Yes.'

'Then you shall certainly see him. He's been asking for you.'

They went into the room together. A nurse ushered them in, and bent over the man in the bed. 'Mr Burnett,' she said softly.

'Oh, please don't wake him!' Glenna protested, moving to the other side.

The girl looked up and smiled. She had a nice smile which transformed her quite ordinary face.

'He needs to see you,' she said. 'He's worried about you. He remembers the explosion, and doesn't know where you were when it happened. Believe me, he'll be much more quickly better, once he knows you're all right.'

'Has he been conscious?' Adrian Burnett asked.

'Briefly. I was with him last night. I've only just come back on duty. He was rambling, mostly, about the explosion and Glenna.' She looked back at Glenna herself. 'He called me by your name all night.'

She looked down again, and gently smoothed a lock of hair away from Ric's forehead. She was nice, Glenna thought, as the nurse called his name again.

Ric opened his eyes, and the nurse stepped back.

'You have visitors.'

He frowned, as though his vision was not quite clear, and as Glenna stepped closer, he put up a wavering hand. As she caught it in hers, he said, 'You're all right! It *is* really you, isn't it? I'm not dreaming this time.'

'You're not dreaming,' she said. 'I'm all right, and I'm here.' His face was pale and scratched; there was a fiery burn on one cheek, and a plaster near the other eye. But he was alive, and his hand was firm and warm and very familiar in hers.

He closed his eyes tightly, and she knew he was holding back tears. 'Oh, *sweet*!' he said, on a long, uneven breath. 'I've been so afraid!'

Adrian Burnett opened the door and ushered the nurse out, joining her in the corridor as Glenna sank down on to the bed and into Ric's unsteady arms.

Afterwards, Adrian Burnett took her and Jane, who had accompanied her to the hospital, out to tea.

'How long have you known my nephew, Miss Lawrence?' he asked.

She told him, and saw the flicker of surprise, quickly hidden, that crossed his face.

'I called your parents and told them what happened,' Jane told her. 'I said we'd be on a train tomorrow.'

'But I can't go home tomorrow!' Glenna exclaimed. She had quite forgotten they were expected home today.

Adrian Burnett looked at her sharply, and Jane gaped.

'I'll ring my parents and explain,' Glenna said. 'I'm sorry, Jane, I'm not going home with you.'

'Am I permitted to ask why not?' asked Ric's uncle.

'Ric needs me,' she said.

He looked at her thoughtfully. Deliberately he put down the spoon he had been stirring his tea with, and asked, 'How well do you know Ric, Miss Lawrence?'

She didn't answer at once, and Jane, sensing some tension, said with slight indignation, 'Look, Mr Burnett, if you mean what I think you mean, I can tell you Glenna isn't like that.'

'I didn't think for a moment that she was,' he said, casting Jane a slightly impatient smile. 'I assure you that I didn't mean anything of the sort. You said, Miss Lawrence, that you've known Ric for only three weeks. You seem to regard yourself as something more than a casual holiday friend, however. Believe me, this is not just idle curiosity. I *need* to know what the relationship is between you two.'

She believed him. 'I can't speak for Ric,' she said, being as honest as she could. 'But I love him.'

Jane gasped. Neither of the other two took any notice.

'Three weeks is a very short time to learn to love someone,' Adrian said quietly.

'Yes.'

There was nothing she could add to that. She loved Ric, and she had loved him in less than three weeks, which was a very short time.

'May I take you back to your hotel?' Adrian asked. 'I would like to talk to you some more.'

She shared a room with Jane, but Jane quietly withdrew and left them alone. Adrian took a chair, which was too small for him, and Glenna sat on one of the twin beds.

'What exactly are you planning to do?' he asked her quietly.

'Just stay here as long as Ric needs me.'

'He may be a long time in hospital.'

'Oh—have they told you that? *Oh!*' She realised she had been silly, jumping to the conclusion that he was all right, just because she had been told he wasn't dying. Sudden fear washed over her, making her feel sick and cold. He had looked battered and pale, but he had held her in both his arms, and the outline of his legs had been clearly visible beneath the thin hospital bedding. But he had spent *hours* in the theatre. He was *whole*, but——

'His injuries——' she whispered. 'They operated. They told me he won't die.'

'No, he won't die,' said Adrian. His face reflected tight control on his emotions. 'But you see, Miss Lawrence, some of the fragments which lodged in his back were unable to be removed by the surgery. There are small splinters of metal actually embedded in the spine. They judged it safer to leave them than to try and remove them. And—even as things are, he may never walk again.'

CHAPTER THREE

SHE sat there and let the words echo in her head. Then she said, 'Does he know?'

'No. He's only been conscious for moments at a time, you know.'

He had gone to sleep again in her arms almost as soon as the nurse and Adrian had left the room. 'Yes,' she said.

'He'll be in some pain, and they'll keep him fairly heavily sedated for a day or two, they told me. But when he asks, he'll have to be told.'

'Is that wise?' she asked hesitantly. 'You said he *may* never walk. If he's told that, he may think it's hopeless to try.'

He smiled at her, and it gave her a pang of pleasure and pain, because when he smiled he was very like Ric.

'Miss Lawrence,' he said, 'I know Ric a little better than you, I think. He's all the family I've ever had. There's always been total honesty between us. He's going to want the truth, whatever it is. If we try to keep it from him, he's going to know. And then he may well imagine things are much worse than they actually are. I've told them as soon as he asks questions, he's to be given the exact truth.'

He stood up and walked to the window, looking out for a few moments before turning back to her, to look at her searchingly. Glenna met his gaze steadily, her grey eyes shadowed by the shock and sadness of the news he had just given her.

'What is it?' she asked.

He ran a hand over his hair and sighed. 'Miss Lawrence——'

'Please call me Glenna, Mr Burnett.'

He smiled wryly. 'Thank you. How old are you, Glenna?'

'Nineteen.'

'Nineteen,' he repeated. 'That's very young.'

She didn't answer, but her mouth set stubbornly in a way her family could have told him meant trouble.

'I'm sorry if I've offended you,' he said. 'But it's Ric I'm thinking of.'

'So am I. I want to do anything I can to help, Mr Burnett. I can stay here in London. I'll get a job here.'

'Glenna.'

She looked up at him, and saw the troubled expression on his face. He spoke to her very gently.

'Glenna, you say he needs you. Are you sure about that?'

'You saw—the nurse said——'

'Yes, I saw how relieved he was to see you. The nurse was right. He needed to see you—*then*. But you may be reading more into that than it warrants, my dear ... I gather you two have been fairly constantly in each other's company for the past three weeks. You were together when the explosion took place. It was natural he should think first of your whereabouts when he woke. It isn't necessarily a declaration of undying love.'

Her eyes were wounded.

'I'm not being deliberately hurtful, Glenna, believe me,' Adrian went on. 'But you see, at nineteen, it's one thing to fall in love with a young man who is handsome and healthy. It's something else to keep on loving him when he may be crippled for life. You said you can't speak for Ric. Does that mean he has never said he loves you?'

'That's right,' she admitted. 'But he wanted to keep seeing me.' *Again, and again and again*, he had said.

'But things have *changed*, Glenna! If he does walk again, it could mean months of patience and perseverance. And if he doesn't—well, that's a different ball-game altogether.'

'If he never walks, he'll still be Ric,' she said simply. 'And I will still love him.'

'He'll still be Ric, all right. But will you still love him? At nineteen, one is so *sure*.'

'*I* am. Why are you trying to talk me out of this?'

'Because I'm older than you, and I can see pitfalls you have no inkling of. Ric's never lacked for girl-friends, but none have been really serious, and I can't imagine that they'll be particularly anxious to hold his hand, now. The thing is, Glenna, he may not need you now, but if you stay—he's in a particularly vulnerable position just now. It won't be hard to make him need you, girl. That's just what I'm afraid of—that he'll come to depend on you, and you'll find you can't take it.'

'I can take it,' she answered him.

'Glenna, you're *too young* for this! Probably the best thing you can do for Ric is to get on a train tonight and stay out of his life.'

'I can't do that. I won't walk out on him.'

'Well, if you won't do it now, you damn well had better not do it later, young lady, or you'll have me to answer to!'

Glenna rang her parents and explained as well as she could, being vague about her plans for coming home. 'It depends on how Ric is,' she explained. 'It will be a few days before I can make definite plans.'

'Dear, you've only known this young man a few

weeks, haven't you?' her mother's puzzled voice came over the phone.

'Yes, but you see, he's *hurt*.'

'I know, dear, you explained that. But don't get carried away by a sense of responsibility, will you? You may find you're caught up in something you'll find difficult to get out of.'

'Mother, it isn't like that! I don't want to get out of it.'

'You mean you're fond of him?'

Fond! 'Yes,' she said, and thinking of him, her voice softened. 'Mother, he's special.'

'Oh, my dear!' There was such a wealth of understanding in that that Glenna felt her eyes pricking with tears. 'Does he feel the same about you?'

'I don't know,' she confessed.

There was silence. Then her mother said, slowly, 'Glenna, you've always been a very sensible child. It may sound harsh, but I think it might be wise if you came home now, and didn't see him again, for both your sakes.'

For a moment, Glenna felt betrayed. 'Oh, *Mother!*' she wailed. 'Not you too!'

'Me and who else?' her mother enquired dryly.

'Ric's uncle.'

'I see. And what did he have to say?'

Glenna told her, and she commented, 'He sounds a very sensible man. Have you thought about his advice?'

'I've thought about it.'

'But have no intention of taking it, obviously. When can we expect to see you, then?'

'I may come home for the weekend, but not to stay. I'll let you know.'

'And what about your college course? Your term starts in ten days, doesn't it?'

'Yes, but I—I may want to stay on in London. I'll enquire about a transfer.'

'And if that isn't possible?'

'Then I'll get a job.'

'You mean you'd give up your training?'

'If I have to, yes.'

Her mother sighed. 'Well, do try to come down at the weekend. Do you have enough money?'

Glenna assured her she did, although she might have to find somewhere cheaper after the weekend. She rang off with a sense of despondency. She was getting no help from anyone, it seemed. Well, that made no difference to her determination. She had said she would stay as long as Ric needed her, and come what may, that was what she intended to do.

But she had reckoned without Ric himself.

Adrian had accepted that she was staying, and had even asked her if he might help with her expenses. Touched, she nonetheless refused. If there came a time when Ric didn't want her any longer, she didn't want to be feeling beholden to his only relative.

She had seen Ric three times, each time still lethargic with the effects of the drugs he was being given, but able to smile at her and hold her hand tightly, even though his conversation was slow and disjointed. Sometimes he would drift back into sleep as she sat there, and she was content to watch him until he opened his eyes again and smiled to see her still sitting there.

Adrian visited every evening, but could not come often during the day. No other visitors were allowed during these early days, and Glenna realised she was privileged, and that Adrian could have stopped her. She told him she was grateful.

'There's no need to thank me,' he said. 'Ric wants you. And you just could be right about him needing you, too.'

On her fourth visit, the staff nurse who had woken Ric on the first day waylaid her. 'You'll find a difference in him,' she warned. 'He's not having so many sedatives. He's more awake, but also in some pain at times. We're trying to keep him as calm as possible.'

Glenna recognised a hint. 'I'll try not to excite him,' she smiled.

The nurse smiled too, and Glenna thought again how it transformed her face. 'He's been a little difficult since he saw the doctor this morning,' she said. 'Is he normally a moody sort of person?'

'I—think he might be.' Glenna caught the other's look of surprise, and added, 'We haven't really known each other for very long—only a few weeks, in fact. But we were together when the accident happened. With a friend.'

'I see. You were very lucky, then.'

'Yes. He pushed me away and tried to rescue a child, a little boy who had got too near the fire.'

'Oh, yes, I had heard about that. Here we are.' The nurse pushed open the door of Ric's room. 'A visitor to cheer you up, Mr Burnett.'

'She's nice,' said Glenna, as she approached the bed.

'Staff Nurse Sidney? Yes, she is. And efficient with it. She has a marvellously soothing way with pain.'

She came close to the bed and looked down at him, giving him her hand. He did look different, now. His eyes had lost their blurred look, and his whole face seemed sharper and more defined, as though the skin had tightened over the bones beneath. There was no hint of boyishness in his face now, and with a sharp sense of loss she intuitively knew that never again would she see him looking like a sulky little boy.

'What's the matter?' he asked, watching her expression.

'You look older, somehow,' she confessed.

'I *feel* older,' he told her grimly. 'Pain, you know, separates the boys from the men.'

She looked at him and saw the fear that lurked at the back of his eyes. 'It isn't only pain, though, is it?' she said gently. Her arms went out to him, and he pulled her down on the bed and kissed her fiercely, pushing her head on to the pillow beside him, parting her lips with an arrogant insistence that brooked no resistance.

Not that she gave him any. Knowing he was using her, she gave him back every response he sought from her, willingly and in full measure.

He moved away and fell back with a groan of pain.

'Are you all right?' she asked anxiously, standing up and trying to smooth her tumbled hair.

'Yes,' he said. 'Just a twinge. You shouldn't have let me do that, Glenna. Why did you?'

'You needed it.'

She flickered a glance at him and saw that the fear was gone from his eyes, and smiled faintly with satisfaction. He had needed some strong physical stimulous to drive it away.

'Is it your intention to give me everything I need?' he asked ironically.

'Yes.'

He looked very hard at her. 'I'll tell you what I don't need, Glenna, and that's pity. Especially yours.'

'That's good,' she said almost flippantly. 'Because you won't get it. You're alive and whole, and you're getting the best medical attention possible, and one of these days you'll walk out of here and start bowling the girls over like ninepins again. But until then, I'm afraid you're stuck with me.'

'I've never bowled the girls over like ninepins, and what do you mean, I'm stuck with you? It was nice of you to stick around, but I realise you have a home and family, and a career to think of. From here on, I'll manage on my own, thanks. You just trot on home and get on with your life. When I get out of here I'll look you up.'

'Thanks, but no, thanks. I'm staying here.'

'Don't be silly. Don't you realise it could be months before I'm mobile? You're supposed to be at college—when—next week?'

'Well, I won't be there, will I?'

'The hell you won't!' he said angrily. 'What makes you think I want you here?'

'*You* just did,' she answered pertly, slanting him a sidelong glance.

Ric looked at her with narrowed eyes, and said slowly, 'I'm sorry to disillusion you, my pet, but the fact is, any woman would have done. Unfortunately, Staff Nurse Sidney's professional sympathy doesn't stretch quite that far.'

Glenna had known it, of course, but to have it put into words was hurtful. She turned away, and he looked at her averted profile with exasperation and some tenderness. 'I can't let you do it, you know,' he said. 'I *mustn't*.'

She heard the new note in his voice and turned quickly, but Ric was looking down at the bedcover, and she couldn't see his eyes.

'You can't stop me,' she said softly, and he looked up.

His voice hardened, and he said, 'I can and I will. I promise you, Glenna, if you don't go home tomorrow and go on with your training, I shall simply tell the hospital staff I never want to be visited by you again. I can choose my own visitors, you know. It's one of the few choices still left to me.'

'Very well,' she said, her shoulders drooping in defeat. 'I'll go home, but I'll visit you every weekend. You won't mind *that*?'

'*Mind!*' His voice was rough. 'If that's what you want,' he said more evenly. 'But, Glenna, you're not obligated—I mean, any time you want to stop, I'll understand.'

'I'm not obligated,' she said quietly. 'And neither are you.'

Her family greeted the news with relief. It had been something of a sensation that Glenna, who they all agreed had her head screwed on right if any of them did, could have fallen so hard for anyone that she was prepared to drop her lifelong ambition just to be near him. The situation had been discussed at length, as family affairs invariably were, but not one of them breathed a word of it outside their home.

When Glenna casually announced her change of plan, there was a tactful silence from her brothers and her sister. All eyes turned to their mother, for if anyone had the right and the nerve to enquire into the reasons, it was she.

'I'm glad you changed your mind, dear,' she said mildly.

'*I didn't* change it,' Glenna admitted. '*He*—he said he wouldn't see me if I stayed.'

'Oh, Glenna!' Alison's soft voice throbbed with sympathy. 'Doesn't he care for you at all?'

Glenna's soft mouth curled into a shy smile. 'Of course he cares for me!' she said. 'That's why he insisted on sending me away. You see, he'd just been told that he might never walk, and'—her voice shook a little—'he was frightened, poor darling, that he wouldn't. He's got some silly idea that being in love with a—a cripple would ruin my life.'

'Not so very silly, I should have thought,' her father put in quietly.

She turned to him quickly, her face passionate with

rejection, but her mother interrupted. 'Did he tell you all this, dear?'

'No, of course not! He told me he didn't want me, and that he'd "look me up" when he got out of hospital.' She smiled with sudden humour. 'And that if I didn't come on home, he'd refuse to see me.'

Her family looked at each other in bewilderment.

Tony, with the bluntness of his eighteen years, put it into words. 'Sounds remarkably like a brush-off to me,' he said.

'Yes, doesn't it?' Glenna grinned. 'He did overdo it, rather. I mean, this was the man who changed his flight and cut short his holiday in France last week, just so he could take me out to dinner in London before I came home. And gave every indication that he couldn't wait to see me again. And—and called my name all night, after he was hurt.' Her eyes went wide and dark with memory. 'I don't know if he's in love with me, but don't you see? It isn't possible that he doesn't care *at all*! He cares enough to be *idiotic* about protecting me from my love for him.'

'Does he know how you feel about him?' asked Alison.

'I expect so,' Glenna confessed a little ruefully. 'I haven't tried very hard to hide it.'

She wouldn't, they all thought affectionately. Glenna had a ruthless honesty that defied any sort of prevarication. Glenna in love would see no earthly reason to hide her feelings.

The week went by on leaden feet, and she finally was able to take the train and go back to see Ric. Her family had worried about a place to stay, and Robin had finally remembered that a friend of his had married a girl whose parents left her with a large, unwieldy house which he believed had been turned into some sort of digs. He made some phone calls, and finally traced the friend, and was told that there would be a small room available and it could be had just for weekends, if that was what his sister wanted.

All she wanted was some place to stay which was cheaper than a hotel. But she was aware that her not being with strangers did much to mollify her family's unease. It turned out well, anyway. She liked the young couple who ran the house, and the others were mostly young people, cheerful but not too rowdy, and they made her welcome without being too curious about her weekend visits.

It was the first time she had been away from Ric for so long since she had met him, and she felt oddly shy as she pushed open the door of the room.

There was a small boy sitting on the visitor's chair by the bed, and as he looked up and smiled at her she experienced a sick shock, because she recognised his little face and dark eyes. She had not thought of the boy at the next table in the restaurant since the night of the explosion. And here he was, smiling at her again with that hint of mischief she had noticed before.

'Hallo,' he said, and started to pick up a pair of crutches that had been propped against the bed, and lever himself up.

'Oh, please don't——' she began, but he grinned.

'I've just been keepin' 'im comp'ny till you came. He saved my life, y' know.'

'Did he? I didn't know.'

'This is Jimmy, Glenna,' Ric said quietly. 'Jimmy, meet Miss Lawrence.'

The boy's accent was unexpected, for he had a foreign look, but his voice was pure London. 'You was there, wasn't yer?' he said. 'W'en I got this——' his eyes went down towards the bottoms of his striped pyjamas, and she saw that only one slippered foot stood between the crutches.

The shock must have shown in her face, for he said kindly, 'Not to worry, though. They're makin' me a plastic one, see. Works just about as good as a real one, they reckon.'

He swung himself towards the door, and she hurried over and opened it for him. 'Ta,' he said. 'W'en I get me plastic foot, I won't need these,' he indicated the crutches. 'Then I'll be able to open doors for *you*.'

'You'd better sit down before you faint,' Ric said curtly, as Glenna closed the door.

'I'm not going to faint,' she said calmly, but she sat down all the same.

'You've gone as pale as these blasted bedsheets,' he told her roughly. 'Was it the crutches, or the thought of the amputation?'

'Neither. I'd only heard that his foot was injured. I didn't know he'd lost it. And seeing him brought back that night. You *did* save his life, didn't you? I couldn't see what happened, you know.'

'It wasn't so heroic. I meant to get him out of the way, and when the explosion came I just automatically threw him down on the ground.'

'And got on top of him?'

'How did you guess?' Humour gleamed for a moment in his eyes. 'I've obviously watched too much TV. It was purely instinctive. Women and children first must be embedded in my subconscious.'

'There were other people around who might have got him out of the way—his parents were there somewhere. Why should you risk *your* life? You didn't even know him.'

'You said he was a nice little boy, and perhaps I thought that made him worth saving.' He sounded serious, but the smile was still in his eyes, answered by the one in hers. He added lightly, 'At the time there was no thinking involved. I just dived.'

'Giving *me* a hearty shove out of the way first.'

'Purely instinct, as I said. Anyway, he *is* a nice boy, and I rather enjoy having him sneak up here occasionally to hero-worship me. That's something that I don't get enough of.'

'Well, you *would* send me away,' she said dulcetly.

'I don't want hero-worship from you.'

'What do you want from me?'

'Exactly nothing.' The laughter had left his eyes, and they looked curiously bleak.

'I've not really thought about Jimmy,' she said. 'Have you met his parents?'

'Yes, they came in one day, full of guilt for letting him slip away that night.'

'They couldn't be blamed. There was such a crowd.'

'Were they grateful to you?'

'Embarrassingly so. Do you mind if we change the subject?'

She smiled, and obliged. 'Are you feeling better?'

'Gradually. And I don't particularly want to talk about the state of my health, either.'

'You're hard to please. Have you had many visitors?' There was a row of Get Well cards adorning the windowsill, and an arrangement of dried leaves and spiky flowers and a bowl of fresh fruit on his bedside table. 'You seem to have been remembered by your friends.'

'I haven't been lonely. Not during visiting hours, anyway.'

'That's good.' Glenna stood up and began fiddling with the bowl of fruit. Some of the grapes were wrinkled and tired-looking. She began breaking them off the brittle stems and dropping them into the rubbish bag provided.

'Have some,' Ric offered. 'I'll never eat all those.'

'No, thanks, I'm not fond of grapes. Have they got *you* on crutches yet?' she asked casually.

'No. And there isn't much likelihood of that either.'

'Why not?' she asked. 'I should have thought that it's a logical first step.'

'Adrian said he told you the diagnosis.'

'Yes, he did.'

'Then you know damn well there may never *be* any first step.'

She turned and looked at him curiously. 'Good heavens! You're the last person I would have taken for a defeatist, and a self-pitying one, at that.'

Fury smouldered briefly in his eyes, then he smiled rather nastily. 'Clever little teacher, aren't you? If coaxing doesn't work, try the goad. You, of all people, should know what a defeatist I am. Don't you remember how we met?'

'That's quite different, and you know it!' she snapped.

'Oh, stop playing the schoolmarm, and come here!' he said irritably, and stretched out a long arm to pull her down on to the bed.

He didn't kiss her, but held her close, his face against her hair. After a while she felt the tension leave his body, and he took a long breath and let it out slowly in a deep sigh.

She stirred and moved her head to look up into his face. There was tenderness in his eyes, and he said, 'Thanks for coming, Glenna. It was sweet of you.'

'I only came because I want to,' she said.

'Promise me that's the only reason you'll ever come,' he said. 'Never out of pity, or duty.'

'I promise,' she said, smiling because he was so absurd and so frightened.

His fingers tangled gently in her hair, and he kissed her, light and sweet. She smiled hazily at him and rested her head on his chest.

Minutes later, he stirred, and she sat up anxiously. 'Am I hurting you?'

'No, of course not. A slight cramp, that's all.' He eased himself up on the pillows. 'That's better.' He put out his hand and Glenna put hers into it.

'Ric,' she said.

'Mm?'

'Please tell me, are you making progress as you should?'

'One leg won't move at all,' he said soberly. 'The other is "responding to stimulus" as they call it. They can't say yet whether I'll be able to walk. If I ever do, I shall probably need—help.'

'You mean crutches?' she said matter-of-factly.

'You call a spade a spade, don't you?'

'Why not? I don't suppose anyone likes the idea of using crutches, but if they help you get about, you'll just have to get used to it, won't you?'

'Shall I?' he said bitterly. 'Well, the question may never arise. They certainly can't put me on crutches the way I am now.'

'But you won't always be this way. They are doing things for your legs, aren't they? Exercises and things?'

'Oh, yes,' he said impatiently. 'Intensive physio-therapy every day.'

'Well, then.'

'Well, then, what?' he mocked. 'When they've done all they can, do I look forward to a lifetime of getting myself from place to place on *crutches*?'

'Ric,' she said gently, 'lots of other people do.'

He closed his eyes wearily. 'Yes, I know. I know. And I suppose they all felt like this at one time. I know I'm lucky if I'm going to be mobile at all. I suppose in time I'll get used to the idea.'

'Maybe you shouldn't.'

'What do you mean?'

'It isn't inevitable, is it? Maybe you should—set your sights higher. Make up your mind that you're going to walk, eventually, without help. On your own two feet. You could.'

'What great faith you have in me.' His hand played with her hair.

'Please try, Ric,' she begged.

'For you?'

She shook her head. 'I haven't the right to ask anything of you, for me. No obligations, remember? Do it for yourself.'

'I don't know that I'm worth it.'

'I do.'

He gave a soft little laugh. 'It's going to be a long, hard slog.'

'I know. I'll help if I can.'

He smiled wryly. 'I don't suppose for a minute that I could do it without you.'

CHAPTER FOUR

SOMETIMES there were other visitors, usually in pairs or groups. If they were there before her, Glenna would wait until they had gone before making her appearance in Ric's room. If they came while she was there, she would politely acknowledge introductions and greetings, and quietly leave soon afterwards. She had found out where Jimmy was, and sometimes visited him, when Ric's room was occupied.

'Don't you like my friends?' Ric said to her one day, after a group of them had gone, and she had slipped back for a few minutes from Jimmy's room.

'That's an odd question.'

'Well?'

'How can I like or dislike them, collectively, like that? They're all individual people. Anyway, I don't know them, really, do I?'

'Because you never stay long enough to get to know them, do you?'

'They come to see you, not me. And it isn't good for you to have too many visitors at a time.'

'Who says?' he asked rudely. 'You sound like one of the nurses—the bossy one with the superiority complex. Don't you like me having other visitors? Are you jealous?'

'Don't be silly,' she said with determined calm. 'It's just that too many of them at once are bad for you.'

'In what way?'

'For one thing, they make you bad-tempered!'

Ric looked at her furiously, and then gave an exasperated little laugh.

'Okay, so I'm bad-tempered. Do you want me to apologise?'

'Do you want to?'

'Not specially. What are you going to do about it?'

'What do you want me to do?'

'Can't you guess?' He held out his hand to her. 'Come here.'

She didn't move, and he dropped his hand back on the cover, and said, 'All right, Glenna, I'm sorry. *Now* will you come here—please?'

She went.

Once she opened the door and found he already had one visitor, a girl who was sprawled head and shoulders across the bed, weeping on his chest. Ric's hands were caressing her back, and as Glenna stood hesitating in the doorway, he cast her an unmistakable look of harassed appeal.

Quietly, Glenna closed the door and went in search of Staff Nurse Sidney, whose trim figure she had glimpsed as she came on the ward.

'I'll deal with it,' she said. 'Would you like to wait in the dayroom for ten minutes? I'll give the young lady a cup of tea and send her home.'

When Glenna returned to Ric, he was alone, and scowling. 'Where the hell have you been?' he snapped. 'Couldn't you see I needed help?'

'I didn't think it would be very tactful for me to interfere,' she said. 'I've been waiting in the dayroom for your visitor to go.'

'Waiting in the dayroom? Couldn't you have *done* something? You've constituted yourself some sort of guardian angel to me, haven't you? Well—guard me!'

'I'm not a dog! And I did do something. I told Staff Nurse Sidney about the situation. It's her job to deal with things like that. I'm sure she did it beautifully.'

'She did. She sized Marina up in one glance and got her out of here in half a minute, oozing sympathy.'

'What a pretty name.'

'She's a pretty girl.' He looked at her blandly, and then looked slightly put out when she laughed. 'What's funny?'

'I'll bet that's the first time you've called for help when you had a pretty girl in your arms!'

He smiled quizzically, and the last trace of temper left his face. 'Marina has an Italian mother, and she fancies herself in the role of a passionate Latin. A few months ago we were—interested in each other. I think her latest affair has died, and she decided to come and visit her old flame to fill in time. Apparently she hadn't heard that I'm—crippled.'

'Was that why she was crying?'

'So she said. Actually, her emotions are as superficial as they're dramatic. And she knows her eyes look gorgeous drenched in tears. They're very dark, and she doesn't go puffy when she cries, like most women.'

She threw him a quick look, tracing the outline of the pattern on the bedcover, with her finger. 'Have you made many women cry?'

'No, I haven't! I've never made *you* cry, have I?'

She shook her head, not telling him of the number of nights she had finally gone to sleep on a sodden pillow.

'You might credit Marina with some genuine emotion,' she reproached him. 'Do you think that you can really judge a girl's sincerity so easily?'

He caught her restless hand in his. But before he could speak, his uncle pushed open the door and walked into the room. Glenna thought that a fleeting look of relief crossed Ric's face, before he greeted the other man.

She stayed, because Adrian always made it clear that he expected her to, and they liked each other. He had accepted that at least as long as Ric was in hospital, she had a place in his nephew's life, and sometimes he took her out for a coffee after visiting was over, and talked to her about Ric. They found a great deal of comfort in each other, and she had never again seen that trace of hard ruthlessness that had appeared when he had warned her that she would have to deal with him if she ran out on Ric.

They talked easily for a while among the three of them, until Ric irritably threw off the cover and complained of being hot. There was air-conditioning, of course, but the room seemed stuffy, and Adrian investigated the high window to see if he could open it. Staff Nurse Sidney looked in as he climbed on a chair and tried to open the catch.

'I'll do that, Mr Burnett,' she said, walking into the room. 'There's a knack to it.'

Adrian stepped down and helped her up on to the chair in his place, stepping back towards the bed.

'There seems to be something wrong with the air-conditioning,' she said as she fiddled with the catch. 'Quite a number of the patients have complained.'

Standing on the other side of the bed, Glenna had a good view of both her and the two men, who were both watching her. She was reaching up to the catch, her starched white uniform with its firm belt emphasising a neat waist with womanly curves above and below in just the right proportions; and the skirt rising above her knees showed she had slender and very shapely legs.

The room seemed suddenly still and silent, and the

nurse glanced around briefly, and then swung the window open with a small exclamation of satisfaction.

Glenna glanced at Adrian and Ric, and saw that they both wore exactly the same expression—one of deeply male appreciation.

Staff Nurse Sidney turned, and Adrian hurried forward to help her down. She smoothed her apron, looking a little flushed, and murmured a quiet thank you.

'Thank *you*, Staff Nurse,' said Adrian, looking very slightly amused, and a good deal younger than forty-seven. He opened the door for her, and she hurried out.

Glenna rounded on them both indignantly. 'You two!' she said. 'You embarrassed that poor girl.'

'Hardly a girl,' Ric observed mildly. 'She's a few years older than me, actually.'

'How few?' Adrian wanted to know. And 'How do you know?' Glenna demanded, at the same time.

'Three. I asked her.'

'*Was* she embarrassed?' Adrian asked Glenna.

'Of course she was. With the two of you ogling her like that!'

'Ogling?' Ric laughed. 'What a wonderful word!'

'We were just admiring,' Adrian explained patiently. 'The way you admire a painting or a statue that you like.'

'Or a man,' Ric suggested. 'Haven't you ever looked at a man and thought how good-looking he was, and just enjoyed looking?'

Glenna opened her mouth and shut it again, remembering that when she had first seen him that was exactly what she had done. But she would never have shown it so blatantly. 'Not so obviously,' she said at last.

'So what's wrong with being honest about it?' he demanded. 'I like looking at Staff Nurse Sidney. She's a lot better to look at than most of the scenery around here, believe me. I like looking at you, too. Do you mind?'

She flushed and shook her head. Adrian smiled at her and said mildly, 'Don't bully the girl, Ric. I don't know why she puts up with you.'

'She doesn't have to,' Ric said shortly, and his uncle looked at him thoughtfully and then wandered over to the door.

'I think I'll just have a word with that girl,' he said. 'In case Glenna's right. See you later, Ric.'

'He thinks we want to quarrel—or make up,' Ric said. 'Which would you prefer?'

'I hate quarrels.'

'With your family, surely you're used to them? All those children, fairly close in age.'

'Of course we squabbled sometimes, when we were children. But we're all very close, and were, even then, really.'

'Tell me about them,' he asked.

'What do you want to know?'

'Oh, you've told me their ages, and what they work at. But what are they like, as people? Is Alison as pretty as you?'

'Much prettier. Why is it so important to a man how a girl looks?'

'It isn't,' he said at once. 'But it's the first thing most men notice, admittedly. 'Is she as self-sacrificing as you are?'

'I'm not self-sacrificing. What a horrible idea!'

'Is it? You have some pretty horrible ideas about me, then.'

'What on earth do you mean?'

'As if you didn't know,' he grinned.

'I shan't be able to come next week,' Glenna told him.

'Why not?' he asked sharply. Then, 'Don't answer that. I told you any time you don't want to——'

'Oh, do stop being ridiculous, Ric! Of course I want to come! But it's the twins' birthday on Saturday. They're having a party, and we never miss one another's birthdays, if we can help it.'

'I have a birthday soon, too.'

'Do you? When?' She memorised the date and as it was a weekday, began to scheme what she could buy him that might be safely entrusted to the post.

'You're not listening!' he accused her. He had been talking.

'I was thinking of a present for your birthday.'

'That's to make me feel guilty about jumping at you.'

'No, it's true. But you're free to feel guilty if you want to,' she smiled mischievously at him.

'Knowing I have plenty to feel guilty about,' he said wryly.

'That isn't what I meant, and you know it,' she said, sitting on the bed and putting her arms around him.

Ric sighed, and stroked her hair, while she rested her head on his chest. His touch was gentle, and she wished he would always be like this. So often he was difficult and defensive, making her tread warily around his moods. She knew that they were caused by his pain and frustration, and a little by guilt, as well. But she made allowances for all of that, and even the guilt she brought him could be borne if she could prevent him sinking into the apathy of despair, and sometimes bring him comfort and soothe his fears and resentments for a while.

The party was a lively one, as all Lawrence parties were, and with one part of her Glenna enjoyed it, as she always did. But another part of her was aching a little, because Ric was in hospital, and in her mind she pictured him alone and miserable. Which was silly, because he had Adrian, and his other friends, although there had not been so many visitors lately.

She drank a little more than usual, hoping to push her thoughts away. And she flirted mildly with several young men who were quite willing to allow their pleasant, unlined faces to be superimposed on a vision of a dark one, slightly scarred and often harsh with present and remembered pain. Glenna became extremely lively.

When she was on her fourth glass of rum punch, Robin, beset by an older brother's sense of responsibility, remonstrated that she had had quite enough.

'I'm fine,' Glenna told him. 'I'm enjoying myself, and don't worry, I shan't disgrace you.'

'All the same, you'd better stick to lemonade from now on.'

'What's this?' Alison interrupted, coming up to them in time to hear this stricture. 'Laying down the law, Robin? You know Glenna never has more than two glasses of anything alcoholic.'

'She has this time, and it shows,' her brother said.

Alison inspected Glenna's becomingly flushed cheeks and sparkling eyes, with interest. 'Oh, nonsense!' she said impatiently. 'The poor kid's just having a bit of fun for a change. Don't take any notice of him, Glenna. After all, Daddy isn't bothered.'

'*Daddy* retired to a quiet corner in another room with some of his friends, about an hour ago,' Robin reminded her caustically. 'Before Glenna had her third drink.'

'Oh, *really*, Robin, anyone would think she was rolling drunk! So what if she's letting her hair down a bit? She can't come to any harm in her own home——'

Glenna interrupted, 'Alison, please! You don't need to stick up for me, really. Robin's only trying to be helpful.' She downed the remainder of her punch, and handed him her glass, smiling with more than a hint of mischief. 'Could you get me some lemonade, please, Robin?'

Giving her a forgiving grin, he went off to get it for her.

'Idiot!' Alison snorted after his retreating back.

'No, he isn't,' said Glenna. 'He's right. Robin is rather a dear, even if he has a slightly overdeveloped sense of responsibility.'

Alison, who was never angry for long, allowed her lovely face to relax into a smile. 'Oh, I suppose he's not so bad. *I* for one am jolly glad to see you having a bit of fun, Glenna. You've done nothing lately but go to your classes and study your books, and drag up to London every weekend to visit your mysterious boy-friend in his dreary hospital.'

'There's nothing *mysterious* about Ric!' Glenna protested laughingly.

'Isn't there? I've noticed you haven't been talking about him much lately.'

'Well, there's not much to talk about when a person is in hospital, is there?'

The strained look which Glenna wore too often these days flitted across her face, and Alison, mentally cursing herself for her tactlessness, said gaily, 'Well, forget about it all just for tonight. Enjoy yourself.'

Forget him, Glenna thought. *Not possible, Alison, dear.* But she allowed herself to be dragged into a rowdy and decidedly childish game involving a complicated system of ridiculous forfeits, and for the rest of the evening devoted herself wholeheartedly to enjoying the party.

She got through it unscathed and undisgraced, to Robin's relief, and having slept the sleep of the just, if slightly tipsy, awoke with a throbbing head. What was left of the morning was devoted to clearing away the debris of the party. After a late lunch, Glenna retired again to bed.

When she came down for tea, Robin gave her a knowing grin and enquired solicitously if she felt better.

'Yes, thank you. And please don't say I told you so. I can see you're dying to.'

'It was on the tip of my tongue,' he grinned, 'but I won't. Are you planning to see Ric next weekend?'

'Yes, of course.'

'Alison and I have been invited to spend Saturday night with a friend of mine, and I'll be driving my car. Like a lift?'

Of course she would. It would be better than the tedious train trip, and Robin promised to get her there in time for afternoon visiting.

Disaster struck when they were almost three-quarters of the way there. The engine coughed and died, and they slowly came to a stop as Robin steered the car to the side of the road. The petrol gauge showed the tank held plenty of fuel. Robin cursed, got out and lifted the bonnet. But after fifteen minutes, he conceded defeat.

'Looks like something wrong with the petrol pump,' he said gloomily. 'I'll flag someone down and see if they can take me to a garage. We'll have to get a tow, I'm afraid.'

'But that will take *ages*!' Glenna wailed. 'I've got to get to the hospital.'

'I'm afraid you won't, love.' Robin looked at her with sympathy. 'You'll make it for evening visiting to-night, though.'

'But Ric's expecting me *now*!' She hesitated. 'Perhaps I can get a lift——'

'You can *not*!' her brother said forcefully. 'You'll stay here with Alison, and we'll go on together when the car has been fixed.'

Glenna, about to argue, changed her mind when she looked up at his face. There were times when Robin put his foot down and became utterly immovable, and Glenna suspected that this was one of them.

'Can I come with you to the garage?' she asked. 'I could phone Ric's uncle and explain.'

'I won't leave Alison here alone,' he said. 'I'll phone for you if I can.'

The good Samaritan who stopped for Robin's wave fancied himself as an amateur mechanic, and more precious minutes were lost while he in turn inspected the engine and eventually pronounced himself baffled.

Wriggling with impatience, Glenna finally watched them go off in the other car, Robin taking Adrian's address and promising to find his phone number and try to contact him.

'Did you phone him?' she demanded, the minute her brother returned with a garage truck and driver. 'Was he there?'

'Sorry, he was out. I tried to ring the hospital and give them a message, but the switchboard lost me and I got cut off. I had no more change and the mechanic was waiting.'

Alison, watching Glenna's distressed face, put an arm around her. 'Don't worry, you'll be able to see him and explain tonight. You can wait for a few more hours, can't you?'

'*I* can. It's not *me* that matters—oh, don't you see, Alison? He'll think I'm not coming. I wasn't there last week, and if I don't come now he'll think I'm getting tired of it.'

'But you told him you wouldn't be there last week, didn't you?'

'Yes, but if I don't turn up today, he'll think it was just an excuse.'

'You seem to be doing a lot of assuming about what *he* will think!' said Alison dryly. 'Doesn't he know you better than that by now?'

Glenna's face lightened a little. 'He should, of course. But it's easy to imagine things—to get things out of proportion, when you're more or less chained to a hospital bed, you know.'

'I don't know, fortunately, and I don't see how you can, either.'

'Oh, Alison, I know how he feels!'

'Do you?' her sister asked curiously. 'How do you know?'

'Well——' Glenna hesitated. 'It's because I—oh, intuition, I suppose.'

Alison's lovely mouth opened, and then closed. If she had known several occasions when Glenna's intuition had turned out to be dead wrong, this didn't seem quite the moment to say so.

By the time the garage had repaired the car and they were once more on their way, Glenna was resigned and subdued. No amount of looking at her watch was going to get them there any more quickly, and they were going to arrive at the hospital just in time for evening visiting after stopping for a quick meal.

As they drew into the hospital car park, Alison looked at Robin. 'Well, shall we go and explain to Ric why Glenna couldn't make it this afternoon?'

'Okay,' Robin agreed casually. Taking Glenna's acquiescence for granted, the two of them followed her out of the car. Glenna said nothing. Ric had never said he didn't want to meet her family, or have them visit him. In fact, he had been quite interested in hearing about them. Perhaps, she thought, he would like to meet Alison and Robin.

Besides, she guessed that he was going to be in one of his difficult moods after her unavoidable defection this afternoon, and she was coward enough to hope that their presence would impose some restraint on his temper.

CHAPTER FIVE

GLENNA flew down the corridor and stopped dead at the doorway of Ric's room.

The bed was unoccupied, its covers smooth, the pillows plump and covered with fresh, ironed linen.

Her brother and sister caught up with her as she stepped into the room, and found Ric sitting in the easy chair by the window, closing a book which was lying on his lap.

'Hello, Glenna,' he said casually.

He was wearing a rather elegant-looking robe, and looking strangely different, very handsome and just a little remote. A pair of crutches leaned on the chair beside him. Glenna hesitated, suddenly shy, and he looked past her and smiled. 'You must be Alison,' he said. 'Glenna described you perfectly.'

Glenna had said, *She's much prettier than me*, without describing her sister at all. But the family resemblance was there, so that it wasn't hard for him to guess who she was. And Glenna had never grudged Alison's striking good looks.

Alison smiled back at him, and he told her to sit down, on the only other chair in the room, which she did. Glenna introduced Robin, and the two men shook hands and appraised each other.

'We came to help poor Glenna make her excuses,' Alison told him. 'Robin and I came up to go to a party, so we offered Glenna a lift, to save her that dreary train journey, but unfortunately we broke down.'

'Hard luck,' said Ric. 'But Glenna has no need to make excuses to me. I have no claim on her time, you know.'

'I tried to phone through a message,' Robin said. 'Your uncle was out, and I couldn't get through to the ward.'

'Well, thanks for trying, but it really wasn't that vital, after all.' Ric's voice was mildly amused.

'I told her you would understand,' said Alison. 'I daresay you had heaps of other visitors, anyway.'

He smiled, but didn't answer.

'Did your uncle come?' Glenna asked.

'Not this afternoon. But I expect he'll come in this evening, some time.'

'He did come last weekend, didn't he?'

'Yes, of course. Do stop worrying, Glenna. Marina was here last Sunday, too, as a matter of fact.' Ric smiled at her. 'She held my hand and stroked my brow and cooed. How was the party?'

'Fine,' she told him. Alison, alert at the mention of another female visitor, and missing Glenna's answering grin behind her, decided that his casual attitude to her sister's devotion needed a jolt.

'It was a super party,' she said. 'And Glenna was the life and soul of it, wasn't she, Robin?'

'That's one way of putting it,' Robin said dryly, remembering his anxieties.

'Oh, don't be so stuffy and big-brotherish,' Alison chided. 'Just because the men were buzzing round like flies. What's wrong with a girl letting herself go a bit now and then?'

'They weren't!' exclaimed Glenna, aghast. 'I didn't——'

'Don't be so modest,' Alison laughed blandly. 'At least three of them didn't take their eyes off you all night. And you did have a good time, didn't you?'

'Yes, of course I did. Only——' her eyes flew to Ric, but his face was as bland as her sister's.

'I'm glad you enjoyed it, Glenna,' he said, making her feel like a child being patted on the head. 'And I'll bet,' he added, turning to Alison, 'there was a fair bit of buzzing going on in your direction, too.' He gave her the kind of look which she was very well used to, but her answering smile was cool. He was very attractive, and not at all the pale and peevish invalid who had traded on Glenna's soft heart which she had half expected, but Alison was not here to poach on her sister's preserves.

Ric raised an eyebrow at her a little quizzically, and looked up at Glenna, standing awkwardly beside her brother. 'Why don't you sit on the bed, Glenna?' he asked gently.

'It looks too—perfect. I'm afraid your bossy nurse would be horrified.'

'We must get moving, anyway, Alison,' Robin reminded her. 'We are expected, and we're already late.

Alison agreed, and stood up gracefully.

'It's been nice meeting you both,' Ric said politely. Then, his eyes on Alison, he said, 'Come again.'

Alison didn't answer, but Robin said thanks, and they might do that next time they were in London, and opened the door for his sister.

'You're using crutches,' Glenna said to Ric. 'Are you finding it difficult?'

'It isn't exactly easy, without even one properly working leg. But they tell me there's really nothing to it. I daresay in time I'll get used to them.'

'Not too used to them,' she warned. 'You're going to do without them one day.'

'One day! You're always the little optimist, aren't you?'

'What's the use of being any other way? Crying will get you nowhere.'

'Was I crying?'

'No, of course not.' She wanted to go down beside his chair and lean her head against him and hold his hand, but he was prickly now that the others had gone, and she didn't dare.

Adrian came in, smiling at Glenna with real pleasure. 'We've missed you,' he said. 'Did you enjoy your party?'

'Her sister says she *was* the party,' Ric said lightly.

'Really? Good for you,' Adrian approved. 'I've brought someone to see you, Ric. She and her fiancé are waiting outside. I told them I'd make sure you were presentable.'

'Well, who?' Ric asked with slight impatience.

'Liz Warman.'

Ric's expression didn't alter, but for an instant Glenna thought he went oddly still. 'And fiancé, you said.'

'That's right, she's just got herself engaged, to a Canadian. They flew in this afternoon, en route to her parents' place to break the news, I gather. I picked them up at the airport, which is why I didn't visit you today. I've persuaded them to stay overnight at the flat. Liz would very much like to see you.'

'Help me back to that damned bed,' growled Ric. 'There aren't enough chairs, and Glenna won't sit on the bed. She's afraid Nurse Rogers would have her head.'

Adrian helped him, and Glenna, looking at his face, thought that sitting up had tired him. She hung up his robe and straightened the cover over him as Adrian went to call the visitors. She would have left then, but as she made to move away, he grabbed her wrist in a hard hold to keep her by him.

Liz Warman was a petite, dark-haired beauty with fine pale skin and violet-blue eyes. She kissed Ric and smiled at him, and introduced her Canadian, a tall, fair man who was obviously bursting with pride that he had managed to put a ring on her finger. He was also slightly embarrassed, whether due to natural shyness or because he was so patently fit and healthy when Ric was not, Glenna was unable to decide.

Liz was talkative, in a husky, breathless little voice, and full of her exciting time in Canada over the last six months. Glenna gathered that she had known Ric for a long time, her family being friends of his uncle.

Once, Glenna wriggled her fingers in Ric's hold and tried to withdraw them, but he tightened his grip without looking at her, and she stopped.

Liz was talking about him, now, asking questions and waiting to know when he would be allowed out of the hospital.

'You must come and see us,' she said. 'We'll be staying with my parents for a couple of months.'

'I don't know,' said Ric. 'I could be here longer than that; the doctors are cagey, and I'm still having a lot of physiotherapy. And even when I get out, I may not be getting about very well, you know.'

'But you won't be on crutches for ever, darling!' Liz stopped at the look on his face. 'Oh, Ric, I'm so sorry! But I can't believe that you—Adrian says there's every chance——'

'Of course there is,' said Ric. 'But it's going to be a long time, I'm afraid.'

'Yes, but you'll make it in the end, you'll see.'

Do I sound like that? Glenna wondered, slightly appalled. But no, she couldn't, because Glenna believed with everything within her that Ric would walk again on his own two feet, and it was glaringly obvious that Liz didn't. She desperately wanted to, but she didn't.

Her face mirrored pity and horror behind her concerned optimism, and as she saw that Ric had noticed that too, Glenna began willing her to stop. *Don't pity him*, she wanted to cry. *He can't bear that.*

With relief she heard the signal for the end of visiting time. Liz reluctantly stood up, and her fiancé, with a look of unmistakable relief on his face, picked up the coat she had thrown across the chair and began to help her into it. Ric said it was very good of them to come, and he hoped he would make it to the wedding.

Liz stood buttoning her coat, and Ric turned to Glenna and asked if she was coming again the following day.

'Yes, of course,' she answered. 'I must go now, though.'

He was still holding her hand. Liz dropped a kiss lightly on his mouth, and the Canadian put a proprietorial arm about her shoulder and began to put out his hand to Ric.

Ric either didn't see, or pretended not to. He turned to Glenna, giving her hand a tug. 'What about you, Glenna?' he said, smiling.

She bent to kiss him as Liz had done, but he raised his hand quickly to the back of her head and kept it possessively there, turning it into a lovers' kiss, his lips insistently demanding.

When he finally let her go her cheeks were pink. A quick glance showed her that Liz was looking speculative, and her companion vaguely surprised. Adrian was looking at Ric with a hint of grimness in his expression.

'I'll see you tomorrow,' said Ric. His eyes were bright and rather hard on her face, and Glenna gave him a brief wavery smile and left without saying goodbye.

Glenna spent a restless night, troubled by dreams of a vaguely ominous nature. After a meagre lunch, she returned to the hospital, taking her overnight bag with her, for Robin and Alison were to pick her up immediately the visiting time was over. She hoped that they would not come in to see Ric again. Somehow, yesterday had not gone well. For the first time she hesitated before pushing open the door to Ric's room.

'Jimmy's gone home,' he greeted her. He was sitting up in the bed. The robe he had worn the day before lay across the chair, the crutches propped against it.

'That's great!' she said. 'But you'll miss him.'

'Yes,' said Ric, flicking an unreadable glance at her. 'He promised to visit me. I wonder if he will.'

'I'm sure he will.'

'Always the optimist.' His voice had a faint edge to it. 'Shift those things and sit down.' He gestured towards the chair.

Glenna propped the crutches against the bedside cupboard and lifted the robe, folding it carefully to place on the end of the bed. 'This is nice,' she commented, stroking the rich fabric.

'It was a present.'

It was on the tip of her tongue to ask who from, but she stopped herself.

'From Adrian,' Ric said dryly.

'He's nice, too.' She sat down and smiled up at him. 'Did you like *my* relations?'

'Yes. Your sister doesn't like me, though.'

'Whatever makes you think that?'

'She did. Oh, very politely, but I got the message, right enough.'

'Then you got the wrong message. Alison doesn't take unreasonable dislikes to people.'

'She had damned good reason. I was being cruel to you.'

'Nonsense! You were being very polite,' Glenna protested, but her voice shook a little. She had known she was being subjected to a subtle punishment yesterday, but it had not occurred to her that Alison or Robin would notice.

'Politely cruel,' Ric said, on a note of self-condemnation. 'Your sister is no fool.'

'And she *is* prettier than I am.' Glenna's smile held a hint of mischief.

His look was searching. 'Did that hurt?' he asked abruptly.

'Of course not!' she laughed. 'It's true. I've always been proud of my sister.'

'So that one went wide,' he muttered, half-ruefully. 'You're too nice for words, Glenna.'

'Don't be silly!' She made a face.

'It's not silly. It's true. And it's time I stopped taking advantage of it. I don't want you to come here any more.'

For moments, she was silent with the shock of it. Then she found her voice. 'You don't mean that, Ric! I *can't* stop seeing you. Oh, do stop trying to be so noble!'

'Why not? It's my turn, isn't it? Look, I do mean it, Glenna. You've been very sweet and very faithful, but I don't need you any more. I'm on the mend now. They tell me I'll soon be walking without crutches. Before long I'll be going home, I hope.'

'Have they said that?' she interrupted.

'Yes. And I'm grateful to you, honey. You've helped. It was kind of you——'

'*Kind!*' Her face was stricken.

'Very *kind*,' he reiterated firmly. 'But I won't have you sacrificing yourself any longer. You're young, and very pretty. You should be going to parties every weekend, not visiting a cripple——'

'Wasting away my youth and beauty?' she asked,

suddenly laughing. 'Oh, for heaven's sake, Ric! Next you'll be telling me I'm entitled to a whole man, or something equally hackneyed.'

For a moment she thought he was going to laugh with her. Then a very odd expression crossed his face, and he said deliberately, 'Perhaps you are, at that.'

'What do you mean?'

'You must know that a back injury can affect—other parts of the body.'

She sat very still and looked at him steadily. 'You mean sex.'

He looked at her curiously. Glenna blushed easily, but she wasn't blushing now. If anything, she looked a little pale.

'It wouldn't make any difference,' she said.

'*For God's sake*, Glenna! Of course it would make a difference!'

'I'm sorry!' she said quickly, rising from the chair. 'I meant it wouldn't make any difference to the way I feel about you.'

'You're too young to know what the hell you're talking about!' he told her, suddenly furious. 'A nineteen-year-old virgin with some sort of Florence Nightingale complex!'

'That's a very stupid thing to say!'

'Is it? I'm not so sure about that.' His eyes narrowed. 'The only time I kissed you properly in France, you fought me off. Maybe you feel safer with me this way. If I was impotent, you'd be in no danger, would you?'

She was standing very straight before him, her hands clasped tightly in front of her. 'Are you?' she said.

He looked at her, his mouth twisting in a travesty of a smile. 'No.'

'I'm not frightened of sex,' she said quietly. 'I'm inexperienced, that's all.'

'Well, I'm not in any position to remedy that,' he reminded her bitterly.

Her chin lifted a little. 'I wasn't asking you to. I don't particularly want to—play around before——'

'Before you're married?'

She looked at him with a hint of defiance, and shrugged. 'I just think it should mean something.'

'Yes.'

She wasn't sure what he meant—whether it was acknowledgment of her feelings, or agreement with her principles. Ric had his hand over his eyes, as though he was very tired, or in pain.

Glenna stepped nearer to the bed. 'What is it?' she asked softly.

'Nothing.' He took his hand away. He looked fed up and irritable. 'Glenna, please don't come again.'

That shook her, because there was real pleading in his voice.

'Will you tell me why?' she asked shakily.

'Because,' he said deliberately, 'you're not good for me.' He saw the hurt in her eyes, but went on ruthlessly, 'I don't like myself when you're around. I use you, and you know it.'

'I know. I don't mind.'

'Glenna, I have *nothing* to offer you. Don't you understand?'

'I understand.'

He looked at her in exasperation. 'If you think I need you, you're wrong, you know.'

'You don't need me,' she said. 'But I can help.'

'God in heaven! What do I have to do to make you believe *I don't want you!*'

'You can walk to me on your own two feet, without help, and tell me you want me out of your life. Then I'll believe you.'

Angry dark eyes looked into defiant grey ones. His mouth went firm and hard. 'All right, lady, you've got yourself a deal. I will just damn well do that!'

Glenna sent him books for his birthday—a new novel that was making the best-seller lists, and a beautifully bound book of poetry, ancient and modern, that she found in a dusty, neglected corner of a small old book-shop. She was not a frequent reader of poetry herself, and didn't know if Ric was. But dipping into the pages of the handsome volume, she found snippets that delighted her, and there was such a variety, from translations of the ancient sagas to brief modern witticisms, she thought he would enjoy at least some of it. It was one of those presents that immediately felt right.

When next she saw him, it was sitting on the table beside his bed. There was a bookmark in it.

'I hope you're enjoying it,' she said. 'I didn't know if you like poetry.'

'I find that I do,' he said. 'I'm enjoying it very much. Thank you. And for the other one.' His tone was almost formal.

She found that his mood matched it. He was courteous and cool, and she felt that he was building a wall of invisible ice between them. When his uncle came in, she was relieved. From then on most of the conversation was between the two men. Ric hardly spoke to her, though Adrian made an effort to keep her in the conversation from time to time. Finally he turned and spoke to her directly.

'Did Ric tell you how pleased they are with his progress?' he asked. 'I hear they think he'll soon be dispensing with the crutches, although he may need a stick for a while.'

Glenna looked at Ric. 'Oh, you didn't tell me!'

'Too modest,' Adrian grinned. 'The doctor tells me it's all due to hard work and determination. The physios reckon that most of their patients have to be bullied into practising their walking skills, but Ric here actually has to be made to stop, these days. He's determined to walk as soon as possible.'

'And without any help,' Ric said softly, holding Glenna's eyes with his own. The mockery in his eyes was almost malicious, and it shocked her.

'I know you can do it, Ric,' she said.

'Sure I can. And the sooner the better.'

'That's the spirit,' Adrian beamed, unaware of any undercurrent.

But it was there, and in the ensuing weeks Glenna was increasingly conscious of it. Ric's demeanour towards her was alternately coolly casual and almost savagely mocking. There was no tenderness in his kisses, and she began to avoid them. He said nothing about that, but the hard light in his eyes intensified as she moved away from his touch, and his tongue became so sharp that eventually Adrian intervened.

'That's enough, Ric!' he said harshly, after one of these barbed remarks. 'We know you're under a strain, but you're acting like a spoilt child.'

Ric's eyes turned to his uncle. 'Keep out of this, Adrian. The fact is, I'm not a child any more.'

'That won't stop me from telling you where to get off. You owe Glenna an apology.'

Ric's eyes stayed on the older man's face. 'I apologise, Glenna,' he said.

Adrian's mouth tightened. 'I'll buy you some coffee, Glenna,' he offered, turning to her. 'See you tomorrow, Ric.' He took Glenna's arm and steered her out of the room before she had time to protest.

Over coffee, he said to her, 'Do *you* know what's the matter with him?'

Miserably she shook her head. 'Perhaps I'd better stop coming.'

'Like hell you will.' His voice was quiet, but that didn't fool her. 'I told you at the beginning not to start if you couldn't take it. You're not backing out now.'

'You don't understand,' she told him. 'Ric said he doesn't want me. He told me not to come, and I took no notice.'

'You were right. I have a feeling that if you stop coming, he'll stop trying.'

'I don't know. He made a bargain with me.'

After a moment, Adrian asked, 'Are you going to tell me what it was?'

Glenna shook her head. It was too monstrously hurtful to put into words. 'He *is* much better, isn't he?'

'Physically, yes. But the mental strain is showing in his face, isn't it? And in yours,' he added gently.

She gave him a small smile.

Adrian went on, 'It may be just the strain of trying to walk again. But I can't help feeling there's something else. Don't you have any ideas?'

'One,' she told him reluctantly. 'Was he very fond of Liz Warman?'

'Liz?' His look became intent. 'They've always known each other. From time to time they went about together.' He was thoughtful for a few moments. 'He *has* been different since she visited him, hasn't he?'

'Yes.'

Adrian frowned. 'I've never thought there was anything serious about their relationship. You're not trying to put me off the scent, are you, Glenna?'

'No!' Her astonished look convinced him.

'Never mind,' he smiled, patting her hand on the table. 'We're on the last lap, I'm sure. It won't be long before Ric's back to normal, in every way.'

*

In the end, it was unexpectedly sudden. Glenna had been to the hospital on the weekend, as usual, and on Thursday a small parcel was delivered to her home with an accompanying letter. The package was registered, and her family was curious. She opened it in front of them all.

There was a jewel case, containing a dainty silver filigree bracelet, obviously expensive but not extravagantly so. And a note from Ric.

He had walked out of the hospital, he told her, as he knew she would be glad to hear. He was grateful for the time she had spent with him, and sorry that he had been short-tempered at times. He hoped she would forgive him, and remember him with kindness. The bracelet was to show his appreciation. He wished her well.

It was goodbye. Glenna folded the note again in frozen silence and put it into the box with the bracelet, then took it into her room, leaving her family bewildered.

Later, her mother ventured to go to her. Glenna was standing looking out of the window. 'Read it,' she said indifferently, in answer to her mother's question.

'He might have told you to your face,' Mrs Lawrence commented when she had finished. 'But perhaps he thought this way was kinder.'

'Yes, he might have,' Glenna agreed, replying to the first part of her mother's remark. 'In fact'—she drew a deep breath and turned from the window, her eyes very bright but quite dry—'I think he's going to have to.'

When the taxi dropped her off at the address that Ric had given her months ago, she experienced her first twinge of real nervousness. The apartment building was obviously both exclusive and expensive. When she entered the building and took the lift to the second floor, that became more obvious with every step. The woodwork, the flooring, even the interior of the lift were in such obvious good taste and of the very best of materials. Nothing was ostentatious, but it all spoke discreetly of wealth.

Without thinking of it particularly, because money was not a subject considered especially important by the Lawrences, Glenna had realised that of course Ric and his uncle were a far cry from poor. It had not been obvious in France, but Ric's private room in the hospital, Adrian's car, which she had glimpsed, his clothes, were of the expensive variety. She had, if she thought of it at all, connected the wealth with Adrian rather than his nephew. Now it suddenly occurred to her that Ric might have thought her a gold-digger. Emerging from the lift, she pushed away the thought. Ric was not like that. Neither was he snob enough to think her background unworthy of his—for that thought followed hard on the heels of the other.

Quickly she crossed the thick carpet to a panelled door that bore the number of the Burnetts' apartment. It was opened to her ring by a manservant, and that almost unnerved her.

'I would like to see Mr Burnett,' she said. 'Mr Alaric Burnett.'

He asked for her name, and she hesitated, but gave it. She waited tensely as he went through a door to his right, and then he came back and smiled at her as though he knew she was nervous, and ushered her into a room that was large and elegantly comfortable, with thick carpet and well-buttoned capacious chairs.

Ric was standing by one of them, smiling at her. 'Hello, Glenna. This is a surprise.'

'Is it?' she challenged.

Refusing to take her up on that, he waved her to a chair, and sat down himself. She saw that there was no sign of crutches or a stick. His face looked less thin, but he was a little pale.

'Thank you for the bracelet,' she said.

'I hope you like it.' His gaze flickered over her bare wrists.

'It's beautiful.' The chair was made for relaxing in, deep and soft-cushioned, but she sat tense and straight. 'How are you feeling?'

'Fine. I'm walking a lot. I have very little pain, and the doctors tell me it will pass. Next week I'll be back in my office.' His eyes met hers deliberately. 'I'm really fully recovered.'

'Is that true?'

'Absolutely.'

She searched his face, and had to believe him. 'Then I'm very glad. Why didn't you want to see me again?'

His eyes looked very dark. He was smiling faintly, rather tenderly, at her. 'You never give up, do you?'

'All I want is a reason,' she insisted.

'Even if it hurts?'

'Yes.'

'I would have thought,' he said, after a moment of gazing down at his hands, 'that you'd be glad of a respite from—responsibility.'

'Don't hedge!' she snapped, her voice crisp with exasperation. 'You know very well that I didn't stay by you from a sense of responsibility. Nor from pity.'

'Very well, I know it. And *you* know that I've never said I love you.'

She looked very steadily at him. 'No, you haven't.' *Even if it hurts?* he had asked, just now. Suddenly she was very frightened.

'You see, you would insist on crediting me with some sort of noble motives,' he was saying. 'I'm afraid I'm not that heroic, Glenna. The truth is, among other things, I'm a coward. I didn't want to tell you ...'

'Tell me what?'

'That I'm going to be married.'

Shock held her rigid. His face seemed to recede before her staring eyes, and then come back into focus. It looked stern and rather determined.

'I don't believe you,' she gasped. 'Unless Liz——'

He looked surprised. 'Liz is——' He stopped, as the doorbell rang, and almost immediately there were voices in the hall—the manservant's, and a woman's, vaguely familiar.

'It's all right,' she was saying. 'Just take these through to the kitchen, will you, please. I'm going to try a new recipe. I'll just say hello to Ric before I start.'

Ric stood as she came into the room, and held out his hand to her, drawing her to his side, facing Glenna.

'Ruth, my dear,' he said. 'You remember Glenna? I've just been telling her the good news. Glenna, this is the future Mrs Burnett.'

'Staff Nurse Sidney!' Glenna said stupidly.

'Ruth, *please*!' the woman said, smiling. She looked different with her hair down. And there was a new light in her eyes and colour in her cheeks. On the third finger of her left hand she was wearing a very new diamond ring.

'Ruth,' Glenna managed a stiff smile. 'I hope you're going to be very happy.' At the edge of her vision, she saw Ric's eyebrow rise a fraction, and said hastily, 'I always thought you were the nicest of Ric's nurses. It's wonderful news.'

'Did I hear you say something about a new recipe?' Ric asked, letting go Ruth's hand. 'She's a marvellous cook,' he told Glenna. 'She'd apparently rather come here and make a fantastic meal for Adrian and me than go out for dinner.'

'Why go out and pay the earth for a meal when I can do better myself?' Ruth asked rhetorically. Turning to Glenna, she asked her, 'Have you seen their fabulous kitchen? I can't wait until it's all mine.'

'I always liked domesticated women,' drawled Ric teasingly. 'Get thee to the kitchen, then, and do your stuff.'

Ruth moved away, making a face at him. 'Oh,' she hesitated in the doorway. 'Will Glenna be——'

'Glenna was just about to go,' Ric interrupted smoothly.

Taking the hint, Glenna stood up and echoed his words.

'Well, goodbye, then,' Ruth smiled, and as always, it transformed her face. 'I hope we'll meet again.'

When she had gone, Glenna remained standing. Ric was still looking after Ruth, his face a little tight and strained now that the smile had left it. She recalled the first time she had seen Staff Nurse Sidney, and pain forced the words from her lips. 'Will you call her by my name when she's in your bed?'

His eyes jerked to hers, blazing. '*Shut up*, Glenna!'

Appalled at herself, she closed her eyes for a moment. 'I'm sorry, I'm sorry!'

'You'd better go.'

'Yes.' She moved towards the door, and he didn't follow. In the doorway she turned and saw him standing by the chair, straight and very still and taut. There seemed no expression on his face at all.

Suddenly suspicion leaped. 'I've never seen you walk,' she said. 'We had a deal, remember?'

Seconds ticked away.

'I remember,' he said, and began walking towards her. There was a slight unevenness, a little, almost imperceptible dragging of his left leg. But he walked across the room to her without hesitation, their eyes locked almost in combat. The room was warm, she suddenly realised. There were tiny drops of moisture on his forehead, and her clothes felt clammy on her body. He stood before her, close enough to touch, and said clearly but very quietly, *'Now will you get out of my life?'*

CHAPTER SIX

GLENNA'S family enfolded her under their collective wing. When the first frozen disbelief had passed, they gently manoeuvred her into some sort of social life. One of them was always there to divert attention when her face went small and frightened, as it sometimes did, or to swing her into the gaiety of the crowd when she was looking pensive and lost.

The shadows slowly left her eyes, and the hurt healed until it was only a distant ache that bothered her at unexpected moments. Glenna's strong streak of stubborn common sense and practicality reasserted itself.

She had changed, though. Her mouth had a new firmness and her face was thinner and less girlish. Her face had ceased to reflect openly all her feelings, and she was less quick to show her emotions, more wary of allowing people to know her inmost thoughts.

She was surprised to find that men thought her beautiful. Comparing her face with her sister's warm, golden beauty, her hard-won serenity with Alison's sparkling personality, she laughed disbelievingly at compliments and tended to distrust those who made them.

She had, she thought, been too young to understand her own emotions, and certainly too young to fathom the depths of a man like Ric. Her adolescent love was not enough for him, and he had preferred a mature woman, someone who knew about life and suffering and could fulfil his adult needs. That was what she had to accept, however desperately her instinct fought against it. Her instinct, she told herself firmly over and over, had led her astray. It had blinded her to the fact that Ric did not love her.

A notice of the wedding appeared in the paper. Mr A. A. Burnett of Burnett & Allandale, and Miss Ruth Sidney, had been quietly married in one of London's smaller churches. There was no photograph of the happy couple.

'A. A.?' Alison queried.

'Alaric,' Glenna supplied. It suddenly occurred to her that she had no idea what the second A stood for. How little she had really known him!

Glenna completed her teaching course and found a job in a local school, and her life went on in a fairly predictable way. There were men in it, most of them not serious, but she found that one or two could rouse her to passion. She was relieved, and then wary. Because they were not men that in her cooler moments she could imagine spending the rest of her life with.

Alison married, a quiet young man with receding hair whom she had pursued with unrelenting subtlety. Having no notion that a girl like her could ever be induced to look twice at the likes of him, he had made no moves in her direction until she, intrigued by his unusual lack of apparent interest, gave him unmistakable encouragement. They were very happy.

Robin married, too. At twenty-four, Glenna became restless and took a job in London that appealed to her, because it was working in a school with handicapped children. She remembered a small dark-eyed child called Jimmy, being perky about his 'plastic foot', and she hoped that working with children like him might help her to fill the gap which she sometimes felt existed in her placidly ordered life.

She found the work demanding and rewarding and

was sure that at last she had found satisfaction and serenity, until one day she was strolling through a park. It was Sunday, and there were family parties, feeding the ducks in the small pond, and playing ball games in the open spaces between the trees.

A small boy of about three caught her eyes, because he was good-looking, and there was something about him that looked familiar. As she watched him, he picked up a brightly coloured ball and threw it to a smaller child, a little girl with an enchanting smile, who chased after it and tripped over unsteady feet and fell. The little boy followed and picked her up gently, with much solicitude. It made a touching picture, and Glenna was smiling at it when a woman came into her vision. Her attention was concentrated on the children, and she did not look in Glenna's direction. Glenna was thankful for that. For she was Ruth Sidney—no, Ruth Burnett, she corrected herself painfully—and she was obviously the children's mother.

Somehow, Glenna got herself home to her tiny flatlet before she allowed herself to cry. No wonder the little boy had been familiar—he was like his father. Ric must have looked just like that when he was little.

It was foolish, she told herself, and she exerted every ounce of her common sense trying to push the incident to the back of her mind.

But when she saw an advertisement for teachers to go to New Zealand, it seemed to be aimed just at her. She told herself that she was not running away, that it was the sense of adventure that beckoned her so far away from home and family. She told them she would be back, that it was not for ever. And they didn't try to hold her, for she was twenty-four and a free agent, after all.

So she had come to New Zealand and after a year in a large city school, had moved to the Coromandel and the little home and school for crippled children, where she could put her all into her work, find some pleasure in a few undemanding friendships, and forget for most of the time a dark-eyed man who had once called her name all night, and held her in his arms in the morning, with tears in his eyes.

Except on the anniversary of the day that he had looked coldly into her eyes and told her to get out of his life.

Glenna woke with tears trickling hot down her cheeks. The day was just beginning. The anniversary was over. She got out of bed and busied herself, taking a long shower in her own tiny bathroom, and washing her hair while she was there. She wore it quite long now, because it was easily tied back out of the way, or pinned into a neat bun, and less trouble than having to have it cut and set all the time.

She towelled it vigorously until it was only damp, then combed the tangles out and pinned it into a coil above her nape. The morning was cool, and she put on a cardigan over her pink blouse and wine-red skirt. Flat-heeled shoes completed her dressing. They were comfortable in the classroom and sensible if she should decide to take some of the class outside for a nature walk—for some of them were capable of negotiating the carefully laid paths in the spacious grounds—or for an outdoor game, adapted to their capabilities. She had a great deal of freedom in what she did with her classes, and tried always to keep her programmes as flexible as possible to take advantage of a sunny day, an unexpected happening or a sudden interest shown by the children.

She made herself a light breakfast of cereal, toast and marmalade, and washed up. Then she made her way over to the schoolrooms and began preparing for the day.

As she laid out pencils, made notes on a blackboard and laid exercise books out on desks, working at a leisurely pace, she would not admit to herself that she was merely filling in time until the children arrived for their lessons; keeping herself occupied, and the thoughts at bay.

Eventually they came, some on crutches, surprisingly fast-moving and agile through practice, and others in wheelchairs, negotiating the specially built ramp into the classroom with ease. It was not, in most cases, their disability itself that kept them from going to a normal school with other children. It was the minor traps which an able-bodied world set for those in wheelchairs or on crutches—the steps, stairs, swinging doors which they could not cope with.

In all other respects they were very normal children, the clever ones, the mischievous ones, the quiet ones, just as in any other classroom. There was a slightly wider age-range than in most classes, because of the small numbers. Glenna found that a challenge, and in some ways an asset. It made it easy to divide the class into ability-groups for different subjects. She and Sharon Craig, the other teacher who looked after the smaller children, worked well together. Their ideas on teaching were similar, and although Glenna was the senior, the two of them made a team. Glenna had never found any need to exert authority.

She looked around the classroom, the children seated at their tables which were widely spaced to allow easy access for wheelchairs, and smiled at the young, expectant faces. Almost half of them were Maori or Polynesian children, brown-skinned and with large dark eyes and black hair. The others reflected the variety of

European immigration to New Zealand. Their backgrounds were a mixture, from those whose families had
been among the British first settlers, five or six gener-
ations ago, to children of Dutch and Yugoslav descent,
whose grandparents and perhaps their parents spoke
English with the accent of their homeland. Their skins
ranged from fair and freckled to olive, their hair and
eye colour equally varied.

'Good morning, children,' she greeted them.

'Good morning, Miss Lawrence,' they chorused.

Another day had begun.

Like the rest of the staff, Glenna usually ate in the
communal dining room in the main house. Tonight, as
she entered, she was hailed by Cleo Brent.

'Come and sit here,' Cleo invited her, indicating a
chair at one of the tables for six. Cleo was small and
fair and slightly plump, a lively girl who was very
popular with the rest of the staff. The other girl who
joined them within a few minutes, Peggy Watson, was
also an easy-going type, a freckled brownette whose
slim, strong hands were put to good use in the school's
physiotherapy unit. Glenna had found that in their
company she could regain some of her own teenage
effervescence. All of them got on well with the rest of
the staff, but the three were also special friends. If
Glenna was a little quieter than the other two in
company, when they were alone she was as outgoing as
either of them.

They had disposed of real chicken soup, followed by
a rich mutton stew with vegetables, and were tucking
into home-bottled peaches and custard sauce, when
Peggy asked, 'Have you heard that we might be closing
down?'

Glenna and Cleo looked up from their plates in con-
sternation.

'Who told you that?' Cleo demanded.

'A couple of people. Apparently there's some financial difficulty. You know that the home is administered by a board appointed to execute Helen Duke's will?'

'Yes, of course we know,' said Cleo. 'Glenna and I have both been here a couple of years, you know. We could hardly have missed the annual bunfight and speech-making.'

'Not to mention the weeks of spit-and-polish we all indulge in before the board descends on us for that inspection,' Glenna added. 'And the parents, of course, don't forget them.'

'I'm not forgetting them,' said Cleo. 'But parents visit all the time. The annual hoo-ha is definitely for the board's benefit.'

'Well, some of the board members do visit between times, too,' Glenna reminded her. 'Dr Simons, for instance, the chairman.'

'Yes, of course, dear old Dr Simons,' Cleo agreed, her face lighting with affection. 'But he's almost one of the family.'

'What family?' asked Peggy.

'Well, you know—the school—*us*! Oh, I know it's a cliché, but we *are* almost one big happy family, aren't we? Which reminds me, what's all this about closing down?'

'Well, it seems the trust fund under the will is running out of money.'

'Aren't we all?' Cleo asked gloomily. 'You mean inflation is catching up with the school too?'

'Apparently. But it may be only a rumour.'

'Well, then, let's find out if there's any truth in it,' suggested Glenna practically. She called to a man crossing the dining room on his way out. 'Daniel! Can you spare a minute?'

Daniel Fox M.D., director of the school, stopped

and turned towards their table. As he smiled at them, collectively, his hand resting on the back of an empty chair, she thought Cleo was right, about the family atmosphere here. Everyone, from the director down, was called by their first name when off duty, and sometimes during working hours as well. The informality in no way detracted from the sense of dedication and responsibility which was shared by all the staff.

Daniel Fox, the man with the most responsibility, looked young for the job. He would have been in his late thirties, Glenna guessed, a large, good-looking man with crisp brown hair and shrewd blue eyes which could soften into humour or compassion.

'Well?' he asked now, looking at the three expectant faces in turn, and resting on Glenna's.

'There's a rumour that the school is closing down,' Glenna said without preamble. 'Is it true?'

Daniel pursed his lips and raised his eyes in half mock-wonder, half dismay. He pulled out a chair and sat in it, resting his elbows on the table. 'Where do you girls get your information?'

'Never mind,' Peggy said seriously. 'The point is, is it true?'

'Not strictly,' he said slowly. 'And I want to know where you heard it, Peggy. I promise it won't mean trouble for anyone.'

Instantly recognising the voice of authority, Peggy told him the names of the two nurses she had heard discussing the matter.

'Thank you. Well, nothing is supposed to be said at this stage, but if there are rumours flying, I'd better tell the staff the true position. I'll call a staff meeting—half an hour from now, in the lounge.'

Rising from his chair, he called for silence in the dining room and announced the meeting, asking those present to relay word to anyone who was missing. Then he smiled briefly at the three girls, and left.

'Now there's a man who doesn't beat about the bush,' Peggy remarked admiringly as she watched him leave.

'And kind with it,' Cleo added. 'I wonder if he was ever married.'

'He was, but she died.'

Cleo and Glenna looked surprised. 'Where *do* you get your information?' they chorused.

Peggy laughed. 'I just keep my ears and eyes open, that's all. I think Sister Jones told me.'

'Ingrid?' Cleo looked impressed. Sister Ingrid Jones, the oldest on the staff, in charge of the nurses, was respected by all of them. 'She used to work with Daniel before, didn't she?'

'Years ago, when he was newly qualified,' Glenna remembered. 'He *says* she still terrifies him.'

They all laughed. Sister Ingrid Jones had a stern look about her iron-grey hair and sharp nose, but in spite of a firmness of manner that intimidated the un-initiated adult, she was known to be unfailingly patient with children. Even though her nurses seldom called her Ingrid to her face, whether off duty or not, she and the director had a very amicable relationship.

When the staff gathered in the lounge half an hour later, it was to discover that Peggy's information was at least partly correct. The board, Daniel told them, was finding it difficult financially. The chairman, Dr Simons, was at present attending a conference in Aus-tralia which was bringing together people from all over the world who were involved in administering charitable institutions. Many of them faced similar difficulties, and it was hoped that some solutions would be forthcoming. At the very least they could swap ideas, some of which might be adapted to the needs of the Helen Duke school. As they knew, it had been the wish of Helen Duke when she died that the school should be open to all. The board had some years ago instituted a fee-paying system, where parents paid what they could afford for their child's keep and education. Some government help was also forthcoming, but the bulk of the money came from a trust fund set up under Helen Duke's will. This was invested and administered by the board, which was finding it more difficult every year. No decision had been made, and every effort was being put into keeping the school open. But the matter of possibly closing was to come up at the next annual general meeting, in two months' time.

He hoped that they would be patient and sensible until then. If the school had to be closed, there would be no immediate action. Everyone would have very adequate notice.

'Well!' Cleo said into the general gloom, after Daniel had finished. 'At least now we know the worst.'

'The worst being that we may all have to find another job in a few months' time?' Peggy queried. 'Or that our poor kids will have to find other schools?'

'Both,' Cleo sighed. 'Oh, it *is* a shame. There's such a crying need for places like this!'

'It hasn't happened yet,' Glenna pointed out. 'Perhaps Dr Simons will come up with something. If there's anything that can be done, trust him to find it.'

'Always the optimist!' commented Peggy, waking an echo from the past.

'No point in looking on the dark side, until it's absolutely necessary,' Glenna rejoined lightly. 'Is there?'

The other two laughed and agreed.

'I've a bottle of champagne in my room,' Peggy said. 'I've been saving it for a special occasion. 'Let's go and open it. We'll drink to optimism!'

The life of the school went on just as before, despite a

slight undercurrent of restlessness which occasionally became apparent.

Summer seemed to be ending early. The brilliant red of the pohutukawa trees that lined the coast began to fade, the blossoms dropping to be swept away by the tide. The gardens around the school were also losing their colour, the hibiscus blooms no longer so profuse, the green trees darkening, and some imported deciduous varieties already beginning to colour in mid-February.

One week-day Dr Simons' car was seen parked outside Daniel's office for several hours, and everyone who passed it reported the fact with interest. Something must be in the wind. Curiosity was rife.

It was soon satisfied. Dr Simons had, as Glenna foretold, come up with something. He had met at the conference a British 'expert', a man who knew about both finance and running an institution. He was a partner in a firm of financiers who ran a series of British homes for the disabled, as a sort of charitable adjunct to the firm. If anyone could give them some ideas about pulling the Helen Duke school out of the red, he could.

Or so Dr Simons thought. He had invited the man to stay in his own holiday cottage on the Coromandel coast, combining a holiday from his apparently ceaseless business and charitable obligations with a look at the Helen Duke School and its finances. Daniel was cautiously optimistic.

'He's supposed to be some sort of financial whizz-kid,' he told Glenna, as she talked with him after his officially announcing the move to the staff. 'It's just possible that what his firm can do in England, we can copy here.'

'But surely the firm starts with a lot of money?'

'So did the Helen Duke Trust. At that, it still has a lot. Only it's dwindling so fast the end is very obvious, unless something is done. The thing is, the way they work it, apparently the institutions eventually manage to do very nicely on income from investments, without having to be continually fed cash from other sources.'

'Sounds too good to be true,' Glenna murmured. 'Let's hope it works out.'

'Let's hope,' he echoed fervently. 'This chap is arriving at the end of the week. Dr Simons is bringing him over on Friday afternoon for a quick look round. He's to stay in Dr Simons' house on the coast. Unfortunately the doctor has to return to Auckland, but he's leaving the books and files on the Trust with the financial whizz-kid, for homework.'

'Someone told me the poor man was supposed to be making this some sort of holiday,' Glenna commented.

Daniel laughed. 'You know our Dr Simons. I daresay he made the prospect sound attractive.'

Glenna laughed, too. They were all very fond of their chairman, who could have charmed the birds from the trees with a mixture of gentle humour and well-disguised but quite unbeatable determination.

Daniel had given strict instructions that nothing special was to be laid on for their guest, on Friday. Dr Simons had told the director firmly that he wanted only to see the ordinary everyday activities of the school.

So Glenna was sitting in a corner of her busy classroom with a group of children, bending over a tide-chart, and explaining it to them, when Daniel came in on Friday afternoon, bringing Dr Simons and the other man with him.

The day had turned nasty, from a drizzly, muggy morning to a tearingly windy afternoon punctuated by savage outbursts of rain. The room was growing dark and she had been thinking of switching on the lights.

At first they didn't see her. Daniel introduced the

visitor to some of the children who were working near the door. They knew Dr Simons, and greeted him as an old friend.

Then Daniel's gaze swept the room, and she rose and went to meet them. She had put on the glasses that she wore for reading and close work, and as she moved across the room, she automatically put up her left hand and took them off.

Daniel smiled at her and took her arm, drawing her towards the man standing near the door. 'And this is our Miss Lawrence, who is responsible for this——' He gestured around the room, bright with colourful drawings and murals, charts and pictures lovingly displayed in every available space.

But the man with him didn't respond to the gesture. His eyes were fixed on the girl before him.

'Glenna,' said Daniel, 'this is Mr Alaric Burnett.'

'I know,' she said calmly. 'Hello, Ric.'

'Glenna.' He had got over his initial shock very quickly. His eyes glanced over her quickly, taking in the pinned-up hair, the glasses in her hand, the flat-heeled shoes. He smiled, and in his eyes she read the teasing message, and smiled a trifle sheepishly back at him.

'You know each other?' Dr Simons was plainly delighted.

'We're old—acquaintances,' Glenna told him, and watched Ric's eyebrows rise a trifle. 'But that isn't why you're here,' she added, glancing round all three. 'Please, let's carry on.'

They looked around, spoke to some of the children. Ric asked intelligent questions and she answered them intelligently, coolly composed. After they had gone, she relaxed and congratulated herself. *I'm over it*, she thought. *He means nothing to me now.* For after the initial shock of his appearance, she had felt nothing at all. She switched on some lights and continued with the lesson.

It proved impossible for Ric and Dr Simons to return to the doctor's beach house that evening. The torrential rain had washed away some of the clay which banked the road back to the main highway, exposing the roots of trees, which had fallen across the road, bringing tons of clay, rock and vegetation with them. Ministry of Works workmen would clear the slip in the morning, but in the meantime, they would have to stay for dinner, and be put up for the night. Daniel decreed that they should sleep in the small hospital wing.

Glenna changed out of her skirt and jersey and put on a fresh blue dress of soft synthetic material, before dinner. Discarding the flatties she had worn all day, she found her nicest high-heeled shoes, dainty sling-backed ones in off-white, which showed off her slim ankles.

When she entered the dining room, Daniel, Ric and Dr Simons were already seated at a table with Sister Ingrid Jones. Daniel rose and insisted that she should sit with them. He pulled out a chair beside Ric, saying that no doubt they would have a lot to talk about.

Ric gave a polite nod in her direction, which she returned with a cool smile.

'I'm sorry,' she said to him quietly, as the others began to talk among themselves. 'They're assuming that because we knew each other once, we'll want to pick up the threads. I'm afraid I can't stop Daniel from foisting me on to you.'

'I'm not complaining. You look very——' He hesitated, looking over her appraisingly.

'Schoolmarmish?' she suggested, with a hint of a grin.

He smiled. 'No, not now.'

'But that's what you thought this afternoon.'

'Actually, I thought you looked exactly like a little girl pretending to be a schoolteacher.'

The arrival of their soup saved her from having to find an answer to that. As she picked up her spoon, he said, 'Tonight, I'd say you're looking very lovely. I've often wondered what you would look like when you matured.'

'Have you?' she whispered. He hadn't wanted to watch the process, though. 'How is Ruth?' she asked.

'When I left, blooming.'

'And Adrian?'

'Very well. He would want to be remembered to you, I'm sure.'

'Thank you.'

Dr Simons spoke to him across the table, and he turned his attention away. She watched his profile covertly, now and then. He had matured, too. At thirty-five he might have passed for a few years older. Although his hair was still dark and thick, there were lines about the hazel-brown eyes and a slight grimness about the firm mouth that had not been there when she had met him. Contrasting his appearance with the elderly Dr Simons, whose round face exuded charm and goodwill to everyone, Glenna thought he had not the look of a philanthropist.

He turned his head, and asked, 'And *your* family? Do you keep in touch?'

She told him that Alison and Robin had married, that Peter and Tony had recently gone off on a hitch-hiking tour of Europe and Asia, which they expected would take them a year.

'Adventurous,' he commented. 'And you're a long way from home. How long have you been in New Zealand?'

'About three years.'

'And you intend to stay?'

'I don't know.'

'You come from a close-knit family. Don't you miss them?'

'Oh, yes, of course I do. But I like it here.'

'You mean you like this country, or this particular place?'

'Both. I shall be very sorry if the school has to close down. We're all looking on you as some sort of saviour, you know.'

'I can't promise anything, you know. I'll do my best.'

'How long has your firm been doing this sort of thing?' she asked.

'Since I came out of hospital. It's a sort of debt-of-gratitude thing, I suppose. People used to make pilgrimages and build shrines when they were cured. I just thought that some of the firm's money could be diverted into something constructive instead of simply making more money, and Adrian agreed.'

'Do you ever see Jimmy?'

'Frequently. He's going to come and work for us when he leaves school.'

They moved into the lounge after coffee, and Glenna deliberately sat away from Ric, choosing a chair beside Daniel's. The conversation ranged widely, and she took her part in it quite easily, but it was Ric who was the centre of attention. Perhaps this was because he was a new face, but she thought that he would always be a dominant personality in any gathering, not because he consciously tried to exert any influence, but because he had some sort of magnetism for other people. Glenna could tell that they all liked him, and she felt again her own attraction towards this man. She was glad he was not likely to stay very long, and she would not have to see very much of him. This afternoon she had congratulated herself on feeling nothing for him. Now she was beginning to realise that all too easily she could fall in love again.

CHAPTER SEVEN

GLENNA woke when the dawn was just beginning to streak the dark sky with light.

The wind had blown itself out and the air was utterly still outside. She felt wide awake and knew she would not sleep. Switching on her bedside lamp, she tried for a while to read, but was unable to concentrate. To her annoyance, thoughts of Ric kept intruding. Ric as he had been last night, talking easily with Daniel and the others, laughing now and then. And Ric as he had been, young and gay in France, then pain-filled and afraid in the first days after the fire. Ric tender and wanting her comfort, then hard and bitter and rejecting, later.

She got up and made a cup of tea, slipped into a pair of old jeans and a jersey, found a pair of rubber-soled shoes and a jacket, and slipped outside.

The light was still dim, but she could see well enough to find her way across the courtyard that was bounded on three sides by the staff flats and the hospital wing, going quietly so as not to wake anyone. She cut across a grassed area to a hillside thickly covered with native bush, tall kahikatea and rimu, even a young kauri or two, and smaller ti-tree and punga ferns. The carefully preserved two acres was invaluable for nature study, and a pleasure to simply walk in. There was a good wide path for the children to use, but there were also a number of rougher side-tracks where the more able-bodied and carefully supervised parties of more mobile children could wander.

Glenna's objective was the top of the hill, from which vantage point it was possible to see the sun rise over the distant sea. She took a steep path which was the quickest route.

But she had reckoned without the recent rain. The path was slippery with mud, and she found her feet sliding from under her. She flung out a hand to grab a branch as she fell, but it was too frail, and broke under her weight. The jagged end whipped up and caught her shoulder, ripping through her jacket and jersey. The pain was piercing, and for a few moments she lay biting on her lip, unheeding of the mud which spattered her clothes.

'Stupid!' she muttered to herself, as she gingerly got up. There was no question now of going to watch the sunrise. Her shoulder throbbed, and she could not tell if it was bleeding. She was wet and muddy all over.

She was almost back to her flat when she began to feel faint. Determined to make it, she took a deep breath and put up a hand to her head as she wandered unsteadily towards her own doorway, but she stumbled over something—a rubbish bin, she realised dimly. It was rubbish collection day, and one of the staff had been farsighted enough to put the bin out the night before.

It made rather a noise, and she hoped she had not wakened anyone. But she suddenly had an overwhelming need to sit down, and did so on a nearby step.

Vaguely she heard a door open behind her, and strong hands lifted her. She was swung into the air and deposited on a sofa, and thankfully closed her eyes.

Gradually the nausea and dizziness receded, and she opened her eyes to find Daniel looking down at her with concern in his blue eyes. He was dressed in a maroon robe over pyjamas, and Glenna said, 'I'm sorry, I woke you up.'

'Never mind,' he said. 'What have you been doing to yourself?'

'I slipped. I went for an early morning walk, to see the sunrise. It was muddy.'

'So I see,' he smiled, looking at her humorously. 'Are you hurt?'

'My shoulder.' She tried to sit up, and winced. He bent to help.

'Let's see.' He slipped off her jacket and dropped it on the fawn carpet.

'Your carpet!' she exclaimed. 'And your sofa. I'm filthy!'

'Never mind that—it'll all clean. We'll have to get rid of this jersey, I'm afraid. Can you get it off while I find something to fix you up with?'

He went off to the bathroom and came back equipped with towels, a basin of water and disinfectant, as well as a small first-aid box.

'Lean forward,' he ordered as she eased off the last sleeve of her jersey. He tucked a towel around her and began gently cleaning the wound. 'Not too bad,' he told her. 'But there's a rather nasty splinter in there. Hold tight.' He drew it out, and Glenna winced on a sharply drawn breath.

'I picked the right doorstep to pass out on, didn't I?' she joked.

'Sure did. If you want to faint, always find a doctor's doorway to faint in.' He put a dressing on and smoothed a plaster with an impersonal, deft touch.

Picking up her muddy, damp jersey, he looked at it doubtfully. There was a large jagged hole in the back, caked with blood and mud. Her jeans, she discovered as she swung her legs to the floor, were in a similar state, except for the blood.

'Go into my bathroom and clean up,' Daniel ordered. 'I'll go and get you some clothes from your flat.'

'Thank you. The dress I was wearing last night is on a chair in my room.'

He gave her a clean towel and went out. By the time he came back a few minutes later, she had stripped off the sodden jeans and washed herself down. Daniel tapped on the door and pushed her blue dress through as he opened the door a fraction.

'I found a pair of shoes, too,' he called.

She zipped up the dress and stepped out of the bathroom, gingerly holding the jeans and her mud-caked shoes in one hand.

'Give those to me,' he said. 'You can get them back when the mud's dried.'

He took them away, and Glenna slipped into the shoes he found, the same high-heeled ones she had worn the night before. She tried to smooth her dishevelled hair a little with her hands, as she waited for him to return.

'I'll make you a cup of tea,' Daniel offered when he came back.

'Oh, no. You've done enough——'

'Doctor's orders. Sit down.'

He was remarkably quick. As she sipped the hot, strong beverage, Glenna smiled at him gratefully over the steaming cup.

'Want to tell me why you felt like an early morning walk?' he asked gently.

She shook her head. About to say that she liked walking in the mornings, she changed her mind. Daniel was not easily fooled, and it would only damage the friendly relationship between them if she pretended with him.

'You know, I was married once,' he told her. 'We were very happy until Alice died. I like to think that the experience taught me something, about people— and understanding. I don't like to see any of my staff unhappy, it affects the atmosphere of the place. Besides, I think that we're all friends here, aren't we?'

Glenna nodded. 'I'm not unhappy.'

'But you were troubled last night.'

She glanced up in surprise at his perception.

'I could feel it,' he told her. 'You were sitting next to me, remember?'

'Do you always know when someone sitting next to you is "troubled"?'

He smiled. 'Not always. But sometimes, when it's someone I'm fond of. I've been working with you for two years, Glenna, and I've sometimes wondered what it was in *your* life that taught you what sorrow is.' As she looked up in surprise, he said, 'I recognised it in you, because I had experienced it myself.'

'He didn't die,' she said, involuntarily.

'A man?'

'Yes,' she sighed, smiling a little wryly. 'A man.'

'Was he married?'

'No—at least, not then. He just didn't want me.'

'He must have been crazy.' He looked at her, and she knew he meant it.

'Thanks, Daniel. You have a wonderful bedside manner,' she teased. Putting down her empty cup, she rose to go.

'Sure you're all right now?' he asked, as he opened the door for her.

'I'm fine. I've had the best of medical attention, after all.' But she shivered a little as she felt the cool air from without.

'Wait,' he said. Reaching behind her, he pulled a sheepskin-lined suede jacket from a peg behind the door and dropped it around her shoulders, pulling the collar together around her throat, so that it rose up behind her head, framing her face. 'You look like a particularly attractive Eskimo,' he said, smiling down at her. He bent and kissed her lips quickly with his mouth firm and warm on hers.

Laughing at the astonishment on her face, he said, 'Highly unethical, I suppose—but then so is treating a patient in my flat, wearing pyjamas.'

He slid his hand under her hair and flicked it out of the jacket, so that it fell around her shoulders. 'There are other men in the world you know, Glenna. Don't waste your life pining for one who hasn't the sense to want you.'

'I don't intend to.' She stepped back from him. 'Thank you for the tea and sympathy.'

Daniel laughed. 'Any time.'

He watched her walk to her own doorway, and when she turned and smiled at him, closed his.

The slip was cleared in the morning, and Dr Simons and Ric left before lunch. Glenna had taken a small group of children outside as part of her language programme. She was encouraging them to feel and describe different textures—grass, tree-bark, buildings, footpaths, leaves.

Glenna watched, smiling, as children wheeled themselves in different directions, or swung on crutches with determination from place to place.

'Close your eyes,' she instructed, 'and think of the feel of things under your hands. 'What word would you use to tell someone about it? Remember how each different surface feels, because later I'm going to ask you to write about it.'

Some of the children groaned good-naturedly at her, but she took no notice. She bent to help a little girl who had wheeled herself too close to a flower bed and got her chair stuck in soft earth, and as she straightened, saw Dr Simons and Ric walking by on their way to the car park, near the front entrance.

Dr Simons smiled and said loudly, for the children's benefit, 'Keeping them all busy, Miss Lawrence? That's the spirit!'

She smiled back, encompassing Ric in her glance, and was taken aback by his unsmiling look in return. His glance flickered over her blouse and skirt, into which she had changed that morning on returning to her own flat, and then back to her face. There was a sort of knowing insolence in his look that was almost contempt. Then the two men passed on, and she told herself she must have imagined it.

On Sunday, Cleo had the day off. She and Glenna drove to Waihi beach for the day, a distance of about seventy miles. The trip took them through the Karangahake gorge, where the narrow road wound round steep cliffs, following the course of a river which flowed beside it. The water, shadowed by a sheer face of grey stone which rose high above it, alternatively flowed smooth and dark, and leaped whitely over stones that littered its bed.

They crossed the river and stopped at a spot where once a thriving township of five thousand people had been settled, in the days of the gold rush. Now only a few houses remained; but for tourists, an enterprising gentleman had set up a gold 'camp' where they could, for a fee, pan their own. One of the old stamper batteries had been restored to operation, and was in motion, crushing the quartz taken from the old mine shaft in the hillside, the resulting dark grey mush being collected into buckets.

Laughing, the two girls took a pan each, and were shown how to take a handful of the gritty grey stuff and gently swirl the pan, washing out the unwanted stone and sand, until only a greenish-golden few grains of the precious metal were left. Watching the unmistakable glitter appear at the bottom of the pan, Glenna began to understand the 'gold fever' which had motivated many men and women to a harsh life on the gold-fields in the last century. She felt a faint stirring of excitement herself.

'We won't get rich on this!' Cleo laughed, carefully pushing her gold into the tiny phial provided for the purpose. 'Look—there's barely a quarter of an inch of it!'

'Mmm, it would take days to get a worthwhile amount,' Glenna agreed. 'And anyway, this is only partly gold, they told us. There's a lot of iron in it, that can be magnetised out later, and silver and other metals as well.'

'They used to have a big plant here to do all that by machine, of course,' said Cleo. 'But this is more fun, even if it won't make us a fortune.'

Glenna agreed. 'Do you think we could bring the children from the school here?' she asked. 'That track we walked down is a bit rough, but wide enough for a vehicle. Perhaps we could get special permission to bring them right in.'

'Mmm, it's a bit uneven,' Cleo said doubtfully, sur-veying the sloping ground about them. 'We'd need all the help we could get. There would be a bit of lifting involved. Let's have a proper look round.'

They did, and decided that the idea was possible, with forethought and care. They determined that on their return they would ask Daniel about it, and per-haps he would get in touch with the proprietor.

At Waihi beach they swam, but carefully. The breakers were inclined to be fierce, unlike the gentle waters of the Thames coast. The surfers with their huge boards were out in force, making the most of the last

warm days for their graceful, fast and sometimes igno-
minious sport. The excitement and pride of the perfectly balanced surfer being carried towards the beach
on the crest of a breaking wave was in marked contrast
to the chagrin of the one hurled head over heels by the
same wave, while his board tossed unguided in the
water beside him.

'*That's* gold?' Daniel said at dinner that evening, when
they expounded their plan to him, and Cleo triumph-
antly produced her phial of hard-won grains.

Cleo picked it up and shook it. It looked for all the
world like blackish grains of sand, with a little muddy
water lying sluggishly at the bottom of it.

'It's supposed to be dried,' she said. 'There are other
metals in it, too. I'll get a magnet and take out the iron,
when it's dried, but the proper purifying process used
mercury, I believe.'

'It certainly looked more like gold when we were
panning it,' Glenna admitted. 'It gleams, in the sun.
The children would love it, Daniel!'

'It would be quite an undertaking, of course. I like
the idea——'

'It would be very educational,' Glenna said eagerly.
'I could build so many programmes round it. History,
a bit of science, plenty of opportunities for creative
language use——'

'Okay! I'm convinced. I'll just have to study the
feasibility of it. Leave it with me. And,' he added, grin-
ning at Cleo, 'let's have a look at this gold of yours
when you've finished drying it and taking out the iron.'

In the event, it was not much different, only, as Cleo
said with wry merriment, there was less of it. Daniel
was unimpressed, and told her so.

'All that glisters is not gold,' he quoted at her

solemnly. Glenna, looking on, grinned sympathetically at Cleo.

'But it *doesn't* glister,' she reminded him. 'That's just the point. If it doesn't, does that mean it *is* gold?'

Daniel raised his eyes to heaven. 'Women! Is that an example of female logic?'

'Not at all!' Cleo retorted. 'The point is, the stuff in here *is* gold, though it may not look like it. Have you seen fool's gold?'

'No. I believe it looks like the real thing.'

'It does. It looks *more* like gold than the real thing— lovely and yellow and glittery. Real gold is sort of greenish, and not nearly so attractive. And yet fool's gold is worth nothing. Funny, isn't it?'

'I have a feeling,' said Daniel, 'that you're propounding some profound truth. Are you?'

'No,' Cleo grinned. 'But there's one there all the same, isn't there, now that you mention it. Aren't there lots of things that seem to be what they're not, and other things that are something better than they seem to be? In life, I mean?' She looked suddenly embarrassed.

'Yes, there certainly are,' said Daniel, quite seriously, looking at her with a certain new respect. 'I believe I detect a sort of greenish glitter about you, Cleo.' He rose and excused himself and went out.

Cleo, looking after him in a slightly bemused fashion, asked, 'Was that a compliment?'

'I think so,' Glenna laughed. 'You're privileged. I don't believe he hands out compliments to members of his staff every day.'

'He was joking, though.'

'I don't think so. Not entirely, anyway. Just accept it gracefully.'

'Well, I haven't much choice, have I?' Cleo said

somewhat resentfully. 'It *was* sort of hit and run, wasn't it?'

Glenna looked at her friend thoughtfully. 'Are you —interested in Daniel?'

'Isn't everyone?' Cleo enquired flippantly.

Glenna looked surprised. 'Are they?'

Cleo looked at her with affection mingled with slight exasperation. 'It's unnatural, you know, the way you are. You're *not* interested, are you? Daniel's the only male around, you know, in this establishment. All the other female staff have at least noticed he's a man.'

'Nonsense. There are several men——'

'None that count!' Cleo insisted. 'One male nurse, who happens to be engaged to another staff member, and anyway, he's barely twenty-one, too young for most of us. The boy who helps the gardener is younger still, and almost completely inarticulate into the bargain. And Mr Newman, who's in charge of the grounds, happens to be fifty if he's a day, and besides, he's married to the cook.'

'Well, don't start turning your fatal charm in *his* direction,' Glenna warned. 'Mrs Newman's meals are one of the reasons I like it here. I'd hate to have her upset.'

Cleo cast her a withering look. 'Apart from the fact that he's married, I'm not that hard up for a man, thanks!'

'I've always thought Mr Newman rather nice,' Glenna said innocently.

'So's my father,' Cleo informed her. 'And he's about the same age, too!'

Glenna found herself regarding Daniel Fox in a new light. As Cleo had pointed out, he was the only personable man in an establishment made up largely of women. Some men would have taken shameless advantage of the fact, but he never had. He was friendly and courteous and occasionally authoritative with his staff, and as far as she could see he treated them all in the same manner. If there was an exception, it would have been Sister Ingrid Jones, and no one in their right minds would have suspected a romantic attachment of any sort between them.

But he was an attractive man, who had once been married. She wondered if he found it a lonely life that he was leading now. She remembered with lingering surprise that he had kissed her once. Sometimes she thought there was an extra warmth in his eyes, since, when he caught hers. But he had never attempted to follow up that fleeting intimacy.

Ric was about quite often, but usually Glenna managed to avoid meeting him. Dr Simons had given him the use of his beach cottage, and left him with papers to study and carte blanche to visit the school and look into its affairs. It was said that he was quietly inspecting every aspect of its running, from the director's office to the spotless confines of Mrs Newman's kitchen.

Inevitably, there were bound to be other occasions when he ate at the school. Once or twice she had seen him at lunch with the director, and she had herself slipped into a chair in an unobtrusive corner of the room, leaving before they were finished.

One Saturday evening, though, Dr Simons was with them and they stopped on the way out and spoke to her. She was sitting alone, because she had been late coming in and Cleo and Peggy had already finished and left. They were going to Thames for the evening, but she had declined an invitation to go with them.

'Dr Fox has been telling us of this interesting idea of yours, to take the children gold-panning,' Dr Simons said.

'I'm going to inspect the place tomorrow, as a matter of fact,' Daniel told her. 'Would you like to come with us?'

Glenna accepted, wondering if Ric was included in the party, but thinking that with Dr Simons and Daniel along, she need not speak to him any more than simple politeness demanded. She would have been at a loose end tomorrow, and to decline would seem churlish and even odd. She risked a fleeting look at Ric, and saw the boredom on his face change for an instant to annoyance. Then he put on a polite smile as Dr Simons said something ponderously chivalrous about 'charming company', and Glenna felt hurt curling inside her. To hide it, she smiled brightly at Daniel and said enthusiastically that she would be looking forward to it.

It was a lie, because from the moment she had glimpsed the anger in Ric's face, she had hoped that something would happen to put paid to the expedition.

Nothing did, however. Daniel knocked on her door at ten the next morning, and the day was bright and sunny. Ric and Dr Simons had arrived, and they were all to go on in Daniel's car together.

Ric sat beside Daniel and Glenna thankfully shared the back seat with the elderly doctor. He, she thought, was another lonely person. His wife had been dead some twelve years, Daniel had once told her, and he filled the gaps with his charitable work. Not only the Helen Duke school, but other committees and institutions benefited from his dedication and generosity with both time and money.

They drove through lushly green farmland, backed by the Coromandel range of mountains, densely covered in thick native bush that was purplish in the distance.

After passing through several small hamlets, sleepy in the sun with their square wooden houses and painted corrugated iron roofs, they skirted Paeroa—

the 'Home of Lemon and Paeroa' as a notice proudly proclaimed. Dr Simons leaned forward and pointed out to Ric the sixteen-foot-high imitation bottle that graced a grassy corner where the road branched off over a bridge.

It was a symbol of the town's one claim to fame—the mineral water which, pumped from its natural spring to a bottling factory and mixed with flavouring, became a popular soft drink, 'Lemon and Paeroa', pale yellow and fizzy and refreshingly different.

Fifteen minutes later they were traversing the rough track leading to the gold-panning venture, sharing it with family parties and a group of American tourists who were drawlingly intrigued by the prospect of gold to take home for a souvenir.

Glenna stayed close to Daniel, showing him the small hut which housed relics and photographs of the old mining days, and taking his arm as they traversed the uneven ground to the race where the gold was washed.

They clambered up the track which ran a few hundred yards up the bush-covered hillside behind the camp site, to see the remains of the huge concrete race which had been used when the gold was plentiful, and big business. The children would not be able to negotiate this, but Dr Simons, intent on showing Ric all that he could, insisted that they should make the short trek, which ended some way inside the old mining shaft, the water-washed floor of which was covered in duckboards for the sightseers.

When they reached the car again, Ric opened the door of the front seat and motioned her in. When she murmured a protest, he smiled with unmistakable mockery, saying, 'Your turn, I insist.'

She turned to Daniel as the car moved over the bridge which spanned the river. 'Well, what do you think?'

'I think the idea is feasible, if we can get enough able-bodied men to help. The wheelchairs would create some difficulties, but if they can be lifted——'

'Oh, that's marvellous. The children will have a wonderful time.'

He looked sideways at her and smiled. 'I thought this was an educational trip?'

'Education can be fun,' she retorted. 'In fact, I think it *should* be enjoyable.'

In the rear, Dr Simons chuckled. 'Times have certainly changed since my day!'

'For the better, I hope,' she smiled at him over her shoulder.

'Oh, decidedly!' he assured her. 'For one thing, the teachers were not nearly so pretty.'

Glenna laughed at that, but didn't reply.

'This trip will need to be on a weekday,' Daniel said. 'I suppose you won't be available, Doctor Simons?'

'No, I'm afraid not. Perhaps Ric here might be willing to help. If Miss Lawrence were to ask him——'

'I'm sorry.' Ric's abrupt reply made Daniel's eyebrows rise a fraction, and Glenna stiffened. Quickly he went on, 'I'm afraid you can't rely on me. It would depend on what stage I've reached with all this paper work Dr Simons has presented me with.'

'We can't leave it too late, or the weather might let us down,' Daniel said easily. 'If we arrange it for the week after next, do you think you might be able to come?'

'I couldn't say for sure. Perhaps I can let you know later.'

'Sure,' Daniel agreed after a brief pause. 'We'll count you as a possible reserve. I'll contact one of the service clubs tomorrow, and see if they can provide a dozen or so strong men for a day. We'll work it out.'

Glenna sat silent. It was obvious to her that Ric had

no intention of coming on the trip. He wanted to avoid her, she realised, just as much as she wanted to avoid him.

Well, if that was the case, they shouldn't find it too difficult to keep their respective distances, she thought wryly.

Strangely, the thought brought her no comfort.

CHAPTER EIGHT

THEY turned over the bridge at Paeroa instead of going straight back home. It was one o'clock, and there was ample time to reach Te Aroha, Daniel said, and swim in the hot mineral pool there.

The town nestled at the foot of a lone mountain after which it was named. From its peak, which held a television transmitter tower which served the Hauraki Plains area roundabout, magnificent views could be seen on a clear day. But they were too late for the mini-bus which transported sightseers to the summit, and none of them professed a strong desire to make the three-hour trek by foot through the thick bush that covered the mountain.

They lunched in a small, bright restaurant. Glenna suggested buying some takeaway foods and picnicking on the rather attractive gardens across the way, but Daniel vetoed that idea.

'You'd be sorry, I'm afraid,' he said. 'Only strangers to these parts picnic in Te Aroha. The warm springs on the mountains are ideal breeding places for sandflies, and you'll find that if you don't keep moving or stay underwater, they'll have a feast off you!'

After their meal, they strolled in the park and admired the mixture of native and imported trees and plants that graced its sloping lawns. Black tuis with white ruffs at their throats called each other from the trees, and even a native pigeon, plump and colourful with its cerise wings and white and green feathers, obligingly sat still for their delighted inspection.

'There's quite a good view from Bald Spur, part-way up the mountain,' Daniel told them. 'The track is quite easy that far. Do you'—glancing round at the other three—'care to try it?'

'How long would it take?' Ric asked.

'Less than an hour,' Daniel assured him.

'I'd like to try it,' said Glenna.

'I think even my old bones could manage that,' Dr Simons smiled.

'Right, let's go.' Daniel turned to lead the way.

By the time they reached Bald Spur, Glenna was panting a little, although they had paused two or three times in the climb through the damp, mossy-smelling bush. Once they had come on a natural depression hollowed out of the rock, where clear water dripped from the stony hillside. Thankfully, Glenna dipped her fingers and wiped some cooling moisture on her forehead. But in spite of the exertion, she was enjoying it.

She leaned on the railing built around the lookout point, and admired the view. The plains were laid out below in a patchwork of fences, hedges and roads, with the rivers creating a winding contrast to the works of mankind.

She turned and looked at Ric, standing looking away from her, and suddenly she experienced a rush of thankfulness that he had been able to make this climb with so little apparent effort, when eight years ago it had been thought he might never walk. His profile showed her an expression that was relaxed and full of quiet enjoyment. He was obviously in no pain, and he had not panted at all, as she had.

It did not matter that she had lost him. It only mattered that he was well and whole and contented with life. In that moment she allowed her love for him to surface from the defensive covering of bitterness and hurt and indifference which she had determinedly built over it, and was filled with a quiet joy that held no pain. Somewhere in her subconscious she was aware that pain would follow the tacit admission that she still loved him, but for the moment there was pure pleasure in his presence and the knowledge of his evident contentment.

He turned, perhaps feeling that she was watching him. He did not smile, but his eyes rested on her darkened grey ones with intentness, holding none of the mockery or latent hostility with which he had lately seemed to regard her.

The moment passed as Daniel touched her arm and pointed out to her some feature of the landscape so far below them. Glenna avoided looking at Ric for more than the most fleeting moments for the rest of the day. She wanted to savour that moment of communion with him, and dreaded the return of the coldness with which he had been treating her since they had met again.

The water in the pool was warm when they entered the main pool-house for the swim. They stayed less than an hour, for too long in mineral water was inclined to sap one of energy. Afterwards they inspected the spring outside where the water bubbled from the ground boiling hot, and sampled the peculiar flavour of the 'health-giving' soda water dispensed by a hand-pump nearby. In the nineteenth century the town had been a very popular health resort, the baths and springs credited with all kinds of curative properties.

As they drove homeward, Dr Simons said, 'You two must come and have dinner with Ric and myself tonight. We went fishing this morning and there are three fine snapper in my fridge. I've sampled your hospitality enough, Daniel. Let me cook you a meal.'

'I can vouch for his culinary ability,' Ric said. 'The

doctor has missed his vocation. He should have been a chef.'

'Well, thanks very much,' said Daniel, with obvious pleasure. 'We'd be delighted, wouldn't we, Glenna?'

Put like that, she could hardly refuse the invitation, she told herself, as she murmured pleased agreement. To be honest, she didn't really want to refuse.

After Ric and the doctor had climbed into their own car and left them, she and Daniel repaired to their own respective quarters to change. After some cogitation, Glenna chose to wear a softly flowing skirt of light wool, slimly fitted over her hips and swirling into a flare about her ankles. It was deep blue, and she wore a blue-grey cross-over jersey silk top with it, with a small spray of artificial violets pinned in the vee of the neckline.

She brushed her hair thoroughly until it gleamed, and pinned it into its usual knot at the nape of her neck. For a moment she was tempted to leave it loose, but she never did, these days, and there was, she told herself, no reason to change her style just for tonight.

Ric opened the front door to them when they arrived, sweeping a comprehensive glance over Glenna as she walked past him into the tiny hallway.

'You look very nice,' he said quietly, and she thanked him calmly for the conventional compliment, hiding the quite unwarranted pleasure it gave her.

'Dr Simons is tied up in the kitchen,' he said, ushering them through the doorway into the small lounge with the dining table in the corner. 'I'm instructed to give you a drink and play host for a while.'

They both accepted a glass of sherry, and Glenna, seating herself on the sofa, was able to smile at Ric quite naturally as she took hers from his hand.

'You do look nice,' Daniel told her, as he raised his glass to her. 'Quite beautiful, in fact.'

Ric, too, made her a silent toast, and she smiled again at them both, looking down at the golden liquid in her glass before taking a sip.

'Very nice,' Ric commented, when he had tasted his. 'What is it?' He glanced at the bottle on the small side table in a corner.

'A local firm makes it,' Daniel told him. 'There are two or three vineyards in the area. Some of their wines are first-class.' He picked up the bottle and passed it to Ric for his inspection. 'Are you a connoisseur?'

'Far from it,' Ric disclaimed. 'But my uncle has tried to educate me to a certain extent. He appreciates the finer points far more than I.'

'Does Adrian still live with you?' Glenna asked idly.

'No.' He seemed to hesitate, as if choosing his words. 'The flat was his, you know. He still lives there, but I bought a house.' Then, as she was preparing to make some remark about how a house was so much better for a family, he turned to Daniel and changed the subject.

So they were not to discuss his family. She was glad, because with the thought of Ruth and those two lovely children, she found that the ache she had endured for years was threatening to start again.

But it was a little odd. Most happily married men were eager to talk about their children, at least. Was he trying to spare her feelings? She stilled at the thought. What a fool she had been this afternoon, letting him see so clearly how she felt. He had, after all, made it brutally clear all those years before that he could never care for her in that way. He must have thought she was throwing her heart at his feet yet again. Had that oddly gentle look of his been pity?

Glenna had learned poise over the years. She cradled her glass loosely in her fingers, sitting apparently relaxed and faintly smiling while the men talked, occasionally injecting a remark herself. But inwardly she

was squirming with embarrassment and self-condemnation. What a fool she was! And he—had he thought
her so infatuated with him that she would throw herself at a married man? Did he imagine she had been
eating her heart out all these years for him, growing
into an old maid because one man had rejected her
love?

Disregarding logic, her mind began to convince her
that Ric was to blame for the chaos of her emotions.

She was relieved when a beaming Dr Simons announced that dinner was ready. Quickly she got up to help
him serve the tomato soup, topped with grated cheese
and parsley, that he had prepared for a first course.

The snapper, filleted, crumbed and fried in butter,
could not be faulted, as the doctor's guests were quick
to tell him. And the cheeseboard that followed, with its
variety of cheeses, both traditional Cheddar and New
Zealand-made versions of continental types, was the
perfect ending to a delicious meal.

'I'm not much of a hand at sweets,' their host apologised.

'I'm not fond of sweets,' Glenna said quickly. 'This
is much better.'

'A truly magnificent meal,' Ric complimented him in
turn.

Glenna saw an opportunity to show Ric that she
really didn't care so much as he thought. Lightly, she
laughed and said, 'That's a compliment indeed, Doctor.
Ric's wife is a superb cook.'

Ric's hand convulsed on the cracker he was holding,
and the biscuit broke into two neat halves, dropping
on to his plate.

'His *wife*?' Dr Simons exclaimed, startled.

'I understood you were a bachelor, Ric,' Daniel remarked, casting the other man a look of mild curiosity.

'Actually, I'm not married, and never have been,'

Ric acknowledged quietly, as he saw embarrassment chase the surprise from his host's face. If there was some secret in Ric's past, the doctor obviously did not relish its discovery at his dinner table.

'But—Ruth.' Glenna heard her own voice as from some miles away.

Ric smiled, his voice calm, his eyes completely unreadable as he watched her face. 'A slight misunderstanding, I think, Glenna. Ruth is married to my uncle.'

'Adrian?'

'Yes. I expect you saw the announcement of the wedding in the paper, and jumped to conclusions. My uncle and I have the same initial,' he explained to the other two men. 'And as we work for the same firm, and lived for a number of years in the same apartment, it led to frequent—mistakes—of this kind. Shortening my name to Ric has helped a little, of course.'

It was no mistake, Glenna was thinking. Her shock was succeeded by immediate compassion for Ric, and indignation that Ruth should have been stolen from him by his uncle.

She thought of the two children she had seen, so like Ric—and so like his uncle, whom he also resembled.

'I'm so sorry, Ric,' she said, sympathy making her voice husky with latent tears. How *could* they have done that to him, when he was barely out of hospital, too?

She saw him look at her in surprise, and then he flushed under his tan, and she realised he was embarrassed. Of course, the other two didn't know that he had been engaged to Ruth before she married his uncle. She had just put her foot in it again. Hastily, she said, 'I hope you'll forgive my silly mistake.'

'Of course,' he said smoothly. 'As I said, it happens

all the time. Adrian and I are quite used to it.'

Glenna offered to make coffee, glad of an excuse to
escape to the kitchen and try to adjust to the shattering
knowledge that Ric was not married, after all.

It didn't make any difference, of course. His patent
lack of interest in herself put him as much out of reach
as if he were married a dozen times over.

Trying to pretend that there was any difference
would only bring her more pain. 'It makes no difference,' she muttered to herself fiercely, as she spooned
coffee into cups. She was pouring boiling water when
Ric appeared in the doorway, and she poured some on
to the table by mistake.

'Here,' he said, taking the electric jug from her hand.
'Have you burned yourself?'

'No, it's only on the table,' she assured him with
what she thought of as remarkable calm. She fetched a
cloth from the sink and mopped up.

'I thought I'd come and help,' he said casually, as he
finished filling the cups. 'The conversation has turned
medical in there.'

'That's kind of you,' she said. 'If you carry your
cup and the sugar, I can put the rest on a tray.'

'Glenna,' he said, his voice held a new hint of
urgency, 'I have to talk to you.'

Her heart seemed to plunge a little. 'Okay,' she
shrugged. 'Talk.'

'Not here,' he said impatiently. 'Will you see me
one night this week? We could have dinner if you like,
and go for a drive afterwards.'

'I—don't think so, thanks.' She bent to pick up the
tray, but he caught her arm before she could grasp it,
and turned her to face him.

She stood rigidly patient in his grasp, her face determinedly calm. His hand dropped from her arm, and he
said, 'Please, Glenna. It's necessary.'

'Not for me,' she said, calmly, distinctly, and not without feeling a certain bitter triumph at being able to refuse him what he wanted.

'There's something I have to——'

He stopped abruptly as Dr Simons entered, saying, 'Did we chase you away, Ric, talking shop? Sorry about that, but if you both come back, we'll promise not to do it again.'

'Not at all,' Ric returned politely. 'I just came to help Glenna with the coffee. I believe it's ready, too.' He picked up the tray himself and waited for her to precede him into the lounge, carrying a cup and the sugar bowl.

Daniel was seated on the sofa, and when everyone had their coffee, she chose to sit beside him, deliberately quite close. Daniel was a comforting person to sit close to, solid and large and so very understanding. He cast her a quick look or two as she bore her part in the conversation with cool composure, and when she leaned forward to put her coffee cup on the low table before them, he laid his arm along the back of the sofa, so that when she leaned back her head was against his sleeve.

Ric was watching them with a hint of speculation in his eyes, and when Glenna stared coolly back at him, she saw a glitter of hostility enter them. *He's jealous*, she thought, with wonder and a little jubilation, quickly succeeded by animosity. He didn't want her himself, but he apparently didn't relish seeing her happy in another man's company. Deliberately, she turned and gave Daniel a small, intimate smile, and he smiled back with what she could have sworn was a glimmer of mischief. Did he know what she was doing? Suddenly despising herself, she made to wriggle a little away from him. But Daniel, without looking at her again, without hesitating in the sentence he was using to Dr Simons, dropped his hand firmly on to her shoulder, with a gentle but quite implacable hold which she could not evade without making it blatantly obvious. And his hand stayed there for the rest of the evening, until he helped her to her feet as they took their leave.

Both Dr Simons and Ric saw them to the door, and as they were standing there saying last farewells, Ric said casually, 'Tuesday evening, then, Glenna? I'll pick you up at six,' as though he was merely checking an arrangement already made. And before she had gathered her wits sufficiently to counter the unexpected move, he nodded to Daniel, said, 'Goodnight, then,' and sauntered back inside.

'Got a date?' Daniel asked casually as he drove the car at a leisurely pace along the winding seaside road.

'Apparently,' she said, unwilling to let him know how she had been outmanoeuvred.

'Does that mean, "mind your own business"?' he asked mildly, flicking her a glance.

'No! Of course not. It's just that I'm not sure if I should have accepted, that's all.'

'Why not? He seems a decent enough bloke. Vouched for by Dr Simons. And you're both free, white and over twenty-one.'

Free. The word seemed to echo in her mind.

As though reading her thoughts, Daniel said, 'You thought he was married.'

'Yes.'

'Well, he isn't. Nobody in their right mind would tell a lie like that to Dr Simons. But I'll get it checked if you like.'

'No. Oh, no! I'm sure it's true,' she said hastily.

'Only it will take you a while to adjust to the idea?'

'Yes, I think it will.'

'Perhaps the outing on Tuesday will help.'

'Perhaps.'

He drove in silence for a while and Glenna tried to calm her thoughts. When they had turned into the road leading to the school, Daniel quietly put his hand out and clamped it gently over the two she was clasping tightly in her lap.

'Ric Burnett is the man in your past, isn't he?' he asked quietly.

Glenna let out a long breath with a trembling little laugh at the end of it. 'Oh, Daniel! You are something else!'

'Am I right?'

'Oh, yes.'

'It wasn't that hard to work out.' He released her hands to turn into the driveway of the school. Drawing up in the car park, he switched off the headlights and turned to face her. 'When a girl like you starts to use a man like me to make some other man jealous, there's got to be something more behind it than the few brief meetings that I know you two have had since Ric has been in New Zealand.'

She was glad of the darkness, because her cheeks were burning. 'Daniel, I'm sorry!' she whispered.

'Think nothing of it, I'm happy to oblige. But that's a dangerous game, on more counts than one, Glenna.'

Before she could answer that, he had got out and came swiftly round to open her door.

He accompanied her to the door of her flat. It opened on to darkness within, and she turned and said, 'Thank you, Daniel, for everything.'

'Don't thank me,' he said. 'Or—do it properly.' His hands reached out and drew her towards him. The irritation that she had sensed beneath his quiet manner surfaced, and he muttered, 'I don't think I'll let you go scot-free after all.'

It was a good deal different from the other time he had kissed her. There was more exasperation than gentleness in it. And there was nothing brief about it. When at last he let her go, he put a finger gently to her shocked mouth, and said, 'I'm sorry, Glenna. You ought to slap my face.'

'I have the impression,' she said, 'that I'm lucky you didn't slap *me*! Was that a punishment?'

'Sort of,' he admitted. 'I did warn you.' He pushed her firmly through the door. 'Go to bed like a good girl. It'll all be over in the morning.'

She stood in her darkened hall and he closed the door decisively behind her. She was still standing there when she heard the door of his own flatlet slam.

CHAPTER NINE

SHE would be out on Tuesday evening, Glenna decided. Tentatively she sounded out Peggy and Cleo to see if they had plans for it, but both declared a firm intention of staying in to watch a television series to which they had become, as Glenna accused them, addicted. There was nothing on in Thames on Tuesday night, they said, except an ancient horror movie which was showing at the only cinema, and why on earth did she want to go out on a Tuesday night, of all nights, anyway? They all had to work in the morning, didn't they?

Glenna mumbled something about feeling restless, and retired defeated from their innocent probing.

As six o'clock approached, she felt more and more trapped. She had debated just taking her little car and going out for a drive on her own, but that seemed a childish thing to do. And she dared not ask Daniel to help her out. For one thing, he had been present when Ric had issued the 'invitation' and so would have obviously demurred at the time if they had had a previous date, and for another, he had shown her that he had no intention of being used by her to protect her from Ric.

After school was out she had changed into jeans and a jersey, washed her hair and busied herself with some long-delayed cleaning about the flat, turning out cupboards and tidying up their contents.

Later, she washed, and tidied her hair, but determined not to be coerced into going out with Ric, she did not change.

At five minutes to six he knocked on the door. Glenna opened it with her lips set firmly in a stubborn line.

His eyes flickered over her without surprise, and he smiled. 'Not ready? I'm only five minutes early, you know. How long will I have to wait?'

'For ever,' she informed him coldly. 'I'm sorry you've had a wasted journey, but I'm not coming.'

'Why?'

'Because,' she answered, anger getting the better of her and making her voice shake, 'I wasn't *invited*——'

'I distinctly remember inviting you to have dinner——'

'And I declined,' she snapped. 'So you tried to trick me into going out with you. Well, it won't work. I'm staying right here.'

She stepped back ready to shut the door, but Ric simply pushed it wider and took it from her hand and shut it as he walked in.

'Okay, we'll stay here and talk,' he said quite gently, but his back was against the door. 'If that's what you prefer.'

'If you don't get out, I'll scream!' she warned.

'Would you?' he asked. 'I haven't touched you, Glenna, and I won't. What will you say when Daniel and half the staff come running? Look, I apologise for coming in uninvited, I apologise for pulling a trick on you the other night, but this is not for my sake, or yours. There's a misunderstanding that I have to clear up. I would rather do it after a decent meal—I'm hungry, if you aren't—but if you prefer, I'll tell you here, and then I'll go.'

'How long will it take?'

'Not all night,' he told her dryly. 'Are you worried about your reputation?'

'Don't be silly!'

'How severe you sound!' he laughed. 'A schoolmarm to the life!'

The teasing light in his eyes was not cruel; it invited her to join his laughter, and against her will she felt the corners of her mouth tugging upward.

He took shameless advantage. 'Come on, Glenna,' he coaxed. 'Put on something pretty and come out with me. Please? I'd really like to give you dinner.'

'The sugar on the pill?'

'Maybe. Will you come?'

Helplessly, she shrugged. 'Sit down,' she said resignedly. 'I'll be twenty minutes.'

'I'll give you half an hour.'

When she emerged from the bedroom exactly twenty-five minutes later, he was not sitting down, but standing and examining one of the prints on her wall.

'Do you like it?' she asked.

He swung round to face her. 'That—or that?' he queried, indicating first the painting, and then her simple, clinging jersey dress.

'The painting,' she answered firmly.

His mouth quirked at her no-nonsense tone, and she herself heard it critically, wondering why he aroused that tone in her so often. Obediently he turned again to the painting. It was large and modern, rather a stark abstract with heavy dark brown lines, intersected by an almost glowing curve of gold.

'Does it have a name?' he asked.

'No.' She refused to help him.

'Without the gold,' he said slowly, 'it would be impossible to live with. That streak of gold seems to symbolise some hope amid all the—harshness.' He turned and looked at her curiously. 'It doesn't go with your personality—as I used to know it.'

She didn't flinch. Her voice was low as she said, 'I've changed. I've grown up.'

'You've grown beautiful.' The sincerity in his voice shook her. *I won't let him turn my emotions inside out again*, she thought desperately, *I won't!* He looked at her dusky pink gown again, noting how the colour deepened the grey of her eyes, and the matching lipstick emphasised the firm curve of her lower lip. That slight hint of voluptuousness was belied by the severe hair-style, giving her an intriguing air of sophistication.

She watched the admiration grow in his eyes, and trepidation and excitement stirred together within her. Was it possible that in eight years she had developed sufficiently as a woman to bring this man to her side, and keep him there?

One thing, she promised herself. This time she would protect her pride. There would be no headlong adolescent honesty. He would not leave her this time nursing a blatantly broken heart.

From one hand she trailed a cobwebby shawl of palest silver-grey wool, and Ric took it from her and put it round her shoulders. 'It's cold outside,' he said, and opened the door. As she waited on the step for him, he glanced back at the picture. 'I think I do like it,' he said.

Over dinner, he refused to discuss the 'misunderstanding'. 'Later,' he told her. 'Just now I want to enjoy my dinner.'

Glenna capitulated, and devoted herself to choosing from the menu placed before them. They both began with an entrée of scallops, succulently sweet and tender in a creamy savoury sauce. Then Glenna chose veal steak with vegetables, and Ric tucked into a plate of lamb chops. He insisted on New Zealand wine to go with their meal, asking the waiter's advice, which was readily given.

'Would you like a sweet?' he asked, pushing aside his empty plate.

'Not for me, thanks,' Glenna smiled. 'But you have one if you like.'

'I'm not fond of sweets, either. Just coffee, I think.'

Afterwards, they drove up the coast. It was still relatively early, and the dying daylight cast a silvery sheen over the sea. Waves rippled sluggishly along the beaches, and the scattered stones that littered them looked very dark.

Night was falling when he drew up under the shadow of a giant pohutukawa, on a patch of grass near the sand.

'Would you like to walk?' he asked, nodding at the beach in front of them.

The car seemed stuffy all of a sudden, and she felt he wanted to postpone their talk a little while longer.

'All right,' she agreed. The sea looked peaceful and calm. Maybe some of that serenity would rub off on them and make what he had to say easier.

The white glimmer of the sand made it easy to avoid the stones, for they showed in black contrast. But Glenna's high-heeled sandals were a nuisance, and she stopped and slipped them off, hooking their thin heel-straps over her fingers, in one hand. The other hand was held in Ric's warm one as they strolled down to the water's edge.

The water hushed softly at their feet, and as they turned to walk along the sand, Glenna lifted her skirt and let the creamy-edged wavelets caress her toes. A few lights winked at them from the opposite shore.

They walked in silence, and then Ric tugged her hand gently and led her to a large flat-topped rock jutting from the sand, a few yards from the water.

He retained her hand as they sat down, and quietly took a deep breath, because now he could no longer delay.

He propped one foot up in front of him and dropped his arm across his knee, rubbing his chin on the back of his hand. 'Sometimes,' he said ruefully, 'I wish I was a smoker. I'm sure a cigarette would help, right now.'

She remained silent, and he stared out to the darkening shimmer of the sea.

'Glenna, I think you gained an impression the other night that Adrian had stolen my girl. I have to explain, because that isn't true, and no one should be allowed to think that of him. He always liked you, and I have no right to let you believe he would do a thing like that. Besides, it gives you a false impression of my situation, and I don't want you to start feeling sorry for me all over again.'

'Does that mean that Ruth was never engaged to you?'

'Never.'

'But it was convenient to pretend that she was. However did you get her to co-operate?'

'I didn't. She knew nothing about it.'

Glenna's head swung sharply. 'But you introduced her to me as——'

'The future Mrs Burnett,' he reminded her. 'Having just told you that I intended to marry. I counted on your assumption that I would mean the future Mrs Ric Burnett, not the future Mrs Adrian Burnett. And on Ruth's assuming that I had told *you* she was marrying my uncle. It was purely a spur-of-the-moment improvisation. You obviously weren't going to believe that I was planning marriage with someone, and Ruth arrived right on cue, sporting a brand new engagement ring and the aura of imminent wedded bliss. It wasn't until afterwards that I thought of all the possible things she might have said which would have let the cat out of the bag.'

'How lucky for you that she didn't!'

'Yes. But my tangled web of deceit eventually caught up with me. I've always felt rather guilty about involving Ruth unwittingly in that little farce. I couldn't have you thinking ill of her, and of Adrian.'

'Even though I'm unlikely to meet either of them again?'

'Is it more unlikely than that you and I should meet again, after all these years, and on the other side of the world?'

'I suppose not. It does seem——'

'Like fate?'

'Good heavens, what a very banal idea!' Glenna said lightly. His hand slackened on hers with surprise, and she withdrew it and stood up. 'I grew out of that kind of romantic daydreaming long ago.'

'Eight years ago?' he asked, standing too.

In the darkness he loomed over her, his eyes gleaming but unreadable.

'Well, let's say you helped,' she said condescendingly, for there was no point in pretending not to understand his meaning. 'Poor Ric, how very embarrassing you found my adolescent passion. I do apologise for my girlish folly.'

'Was that what it was?' he asked, striding after her as she began walking back along the beach.

'That's what you thought, wasn't it?' she countered, the faintest tinge of bitterness underlying her determined amusement.

'No.'

'Well, whatever did you think, then? That you were the object of my undying love?' She laughed convincingly.

'Not that, either,' he said harshly.

'Well, whatever you believed,' she said, 'you went to a great deal of trouble to finally convince me that my —devotion—was the greatest nuisance to you.'

'Glenna!' He caught at her arm as she made to turn towards the car, and pulled her round to face him. 'It was not a *nuisance*. Your—devotion, if that's what you call it, was very precious to me. But hopeless. I didn't want to hurt you, believe me.' She believed him, because there was pain in his voice. 'But you were so very —so gallantly determined. I know I was brutal at the end. Forgive me.'

'There's nothing to forgive, Ric. I put you in an impossible position. Everyone said I was far too young, and they were right. Now, if you've finished your great confession, could we go back to the car? I'm getting cold.'

'Sure, teacher,' he said dryly, releasing her arm.

In the car, he switched on the interior light and turned a searching look on her face. Glenna returned it with an unflinching one of cool enquiry.

'Your emotions used to show in your face,' he said quietly. 'Now I don't know what you're really thinking.'

'One's emotions are apt to be rather obvious when one is young,' she answered. 'They're so intense.'

'You're not middle-aged, for heaven's sake!' he said irritably. 'Are you telling me you're not capable of any intensity of feeling any more?'

'Perhaps.' She turned a cold profile to him.

'I'm tempted to put that to the test.'

A knot of fear clenched her stomach muscles, but she stayed utterly still and expressionless.

'Once you would have blushed at that,' he said softly, watching her face mercilessly.

She didn't answer. After a few seconds, Ric switched off the light and began to start the car. Glenna pulled her shawl more tightly round her shoulders and held it in front of her breasts with a clenched hand.

He saw her to her door, and she thanked him formally for the meal, not asking him in.

'Will you let me take you out again?' he asked.

She had both hoped for and dreaded this. Her wounded pride had been inevitably resurrected to-night, when he had confessed to a desperate deception resorted to in order to rid himself of her young love. Yet in fairness, she knew he had had little choice.

'I think I need notice of that question,' she said. Then, watching the sudden narrowing of his eyes and realising she might sound coy, she said hastily, 'I mean, you've made your explanations. There's no need to feel obliged to ask me out again.'

'We had an agreement, a long time ago,' he said. 'About no obligations on either side, remember? Do you think we might renew it?'

Hesitantly, because she wasn't at all sure what such an agreement might come to mean if she was to keep seeing him, she said, 'Yes, I suppose so.'

'Fine. Then how about next Saturday? Dr Simons says he won't be able to make it until Sunday, and I'd like to take a day off from paperwork and see something of the countryside. They tell me the other side of Coromandel is something to see. Ever been there?'

'Once. You can make a round trip and come back another way. It's a day trip.'

'Fine. Can I pick you up at eight?'

'Very well. Thank you.'

'Very prettily said,' he teased.

'Goodnight.' She turned to the door, but he got to the handle before her, and opened it wide.

'Goodnight.' He was down the step before she had time to shut the door.

Peggy looked at her curiously over lunch the following day. 'That was a sudden date you had last night, wasn't it?'

Glenna, caught unawares, said, 'Not really. Ric asked me on Sunday to go out with him, when Daniel took me with them to see the gold camp.'

'But if he asked you then, why were you looking for other company last night? Yesterday at lunchtime you were trying to persuade us to go to some grotty film in Thames.'

'Oh, well, that's a bit embarrassing,' Glenna shrugged. 'Actually, I got the day wrong. When he came, I wasn't ready, and I had to keep him waiting while I dressed. Anyway, how did you know I went out with Ric last night?'

'I saw you going out. There are no secrets in this place, as you know.'

Glenna did know, and she was aware that in the next few days she was the subject of much of the inevitable though certainly not malicious gossip that was generated in a small community. She steered clear of Ric when he came on his short visits so as not to give further fuel to it.

On Friday night she was doing some mending in the communal lounge when Daniel strolled over to sit beside her.

'You look very domesticated,' he smiled, 'for a dedicated career woman.'

'Did I ever say I was that?'

'You sometimes give that impression. Did you enjoy yourself on Tuesday night?'

'Yes, thank you.' She looked up from her task, and asked a little wryly, 'Are you asking on behalf of the staff?'

He raised his brows slightly. 'Actually, I'm asking on behalf of the director.'

'Is my private life your concern?'

'If it affects your happiness, yes.'

'Surely only if it affects my work?'

'Or the atmosphere of the place. With a small staff in an isolated community, it's important that we should be able to get on well.'

'Must we all be happy in order to get on well?'

'Not necessarily. But perhaps we should be able to share our problems.'

Her needle stilled, and she looked at him steadily. 'I don't have a problem, thank you. Except perhaps the rather excessive interest being taken in my private life by other members of the staff.'

'I'm sorry. It's a friendly interest, Glenna.'

Repentant, she said, 'Yes, I know. *I'm* sorry, Daniel. I didn't mean to snap.'

'And *I* didn't mean to pry. Did you know this trip we're planning is practically finalised? We have buses organised, and men laid on to help with the wheelchairs. The date is next week Thursday, if it's fine. Suit you?'

'Yes, fine. I haven't mentioned it to the children yet, in case it didn't come off after all, but we have done some work on the history of the region, and especially of the gold-mines, and the prospectors. They'll be more keen to learn about it all once they know there's a trip involved.'

'Bribery? Is that how you teach them?'

'It's called stimulation of interest,' she informed him severely.

'All right, I'll believe you,' he laughed. 'Personally I think you and Cleo want a good excuse to try your hands at gold-panning again. She tells me the sensation is unique. In the last century she would have been one of the first to join the gold-rush.'

Glenna laughed and, looking up, caught Cleo's eye as she crossed the room. 'Here she is now,' she said as the other girl strolled over to join them. 'Are your ears burning, Cleo? We were just talking about you.'

'Nicely, I hope.' Cleo perched herself on the arm of Daniel's chair, for there wasn't another one handy. 'Don't get up,' she told him as he made to rise. 'I'm quite comfy, thanks.'

'Daniel thinks you've caught gold-fever,' Glenna smiled. 'He says you and I are using the trip as an excuse to go panning again.'

'Oh, dear! And I was hoping we'd pulled the wool over his eyes properly.'

'Seriously, though,' said Daniel, 'I'm glad you thought of it. The children need that kind of stimulation. That's one of the problems of being isolated as we are. The school is really too far from any town. It was an old idea to put a bunch of kids with handicaps in a special milieu, away from the community. The surroundings here are beautiful, but the location was frankly a mistake.'

'I've often thought so,' Cleo agreed. 'You must find it something of a disadvantage, too, Glenna.'

'From a teacher's point of view?' Glenna asked. 'Yes, I have, at times. Even though the children here would be less mobile in a town than others, there would be places we could take them for short trips, that entail a lot of work and organisation from here. And some of the children would do quite well in a normal school, if there was one handy enough. It would be good for them to meet other children in the daytime, even if they had to return to the school to sleep, and perhaps for their physiotherapy.'

'It would also be good for the "normal" children,' Daniel added. 'One of the problems that able-bodied people have is that they don't know how to relate to the handicapped.'

'Yes, so many people tend to treat handicapped adults as children, or as if they were mentally handicapped as well,' said Cleo.

'How odd,' Glenna mused. 'They're people, aren't they?'

'Yes, just like other people for all intents and purposes, except a lack of mobility,' Daniel agreed. 'And a great deal of that problem could be overcome if the community at large learned to cater for its handicapped members, and include them in its life. Simple things like ramps instead of steps could do such a lot for that kind of integration.'

'But this school isn't doing much towards that goal, really, is it?' Cleo asked thoughtfully.

'Not enough,' agreed the director. 'It's something that's always bothered me. The children we have here are all potentially able to live nearly normal lives. We should be preparing them for living in a normal community, regarding themselves as part of it.'

'You mean, not thinking of themselves as freaks because they're disabled?' said Cleo.

'Exactly. When I first started working with the physically handicapped, I met a boy who had been in a wheelchair for fifteen years—he had a war injury which had caught up with him years later. Anway, he was a business man, running a very successful operation involving him in quite a lot of travel. Also president of the local paraplegic games committee, and a keen sportsman—javelin and archery were his forte. And when I met him on the ward, playing cards with one of my patients, and asked him whose patient *he* was, he laughed and said I'd got it wrong. He was not one of the patients, he was visiting with a group of volunteers who dispensed cheer to hospital patients.

'I became friends with him after seeing him around

the wards a few times. He always had plenty of friends, because he was such a powerful character. It was very easy to forget the wheelchair. He just insisted by his every attitude that it didn't matter. Once I tried to tell him how much I admired the way he had overcome his handicap, and what an inspiration he was to my patients. I've never forgotten what he said. "Once I knew it was a wheelchair job," he told me, "I knew I had two choices. I could be a cripple for the rest of my life, or I could be a man who happened to be crippled. I decided to be a man." '

'I know exactly what he meant,' Cleo said soberly. 'I've seen people who just give up when they're disabled, and decide to be cripples. He had a very clear way of putting it, didn't he?'

'He's quite a man. You must meet him some time.'

'Sure. When?' Cleo asked promptly.

Daniel looked up at her, and she said quickly, 'Forget it. I was joking.'

'No,' he said, 'he'd like to meet you. When is your next weekend off?'

'This next one, actually.'

'Right.' Daniel rose from his chair. 'I'll phone Charlie tonight and invite us for Sunday lunch. He lives in Auckland.' He smiled, and overrode her embarrassed protest. 'Don't be silly, Cleo. Charlie will love you, and so will his wife.' His eyes surveyed the girl before him with lazy appreciation. 'She's not in the least jealous,' he added.

Cleo was for once at a loss for words. Taking pity on her, Glenna intervened. 'He's married?'

'Sure,' said Daniel. 'For the second time. His first wife died a long time ago. But five years ago he married again. Susan is a real honey. And his money had nothing to do with it. She just simply adores the guy.'

'Oh, that's nice,' Cleo said with perfect sincerity. 'That's really nice.'

'That a wife should adore her husband?' Daniel asked, tongue in cheek.

'That the feeling should be mutual.'

'I didn't say that.'

'So why did he ask her to marry him?'

'That's a question I've never asked him,' Daniel told her. 'Why don't you ask him yourself when you meet him?' With a brief goodnight, he strolled out.

'Oh, Glenna!' Cleo turned anxious eyes to her friend. 'Why don't I learn to keep my big mouth shut?'

'What's the matter?' asked Glenna. 'You haven't said anything dreadful, have you?'

'Only forced poor Daniel into taking me out for a day.'

'Oh, nonsense. He wouldn't have asked you if he hadn't wanted to.'

'But he thought I was angling for an invitation. He's just too kindhearted to snub anyone, that's all.'

'Rubbish. It was perfectly obvious you were joking. And you told him so. He had no need to snub you, if he didn't want to invite you to meet his friends. Don't you want to go?'

'Yes, of course I do!'

'Well then, stop worrying. Look forward to enjoying yourself, idiot.'

'Yes. Yes, I will. Only I do hope he doesn't feel I've taken advantage.'

'If he does, he's quite capable of telling you so,' Glenna remarked, her voice dry with reminiscence. 'Daniel doesn't take kindly to being used.'

'Are you speaking from experience?' Cleo asked with great curiosity.

Glenna began to gather up her sewing. 'Yes,' she answered crisply. 'But the details are not for publication, I'm afraid. You'll just have to take my word for it.'

Cleo, opening her mouth to protest at this, caught a glimpse of the set of Glenna's mouth, and changed her mind.

CHAPTER TEN

SATURDAY was a beautiful day. Mindful of her own advice to Cleo, Glenna dressed for her day with Ric making a firm resolution to simply enjoy it and give no thought to the future.

When he arrived, he cast an approving eye over her orange shirt and tan wrap-around skirt that covered matching shorts, and gave a tantalising glimpse of tanned leg when she walked. He took from her the duffle bag containing her towel and swimsuit and feeling its weight asked, 'What else have you got in here? The Crown Jewels?'

'Some lunch that Mrs Newman let me scrounge from her kitchen, sunglasses, suntan oil, a book.'

'A *book*?'

She ignored the teasing light in his eyes, and said, 'I hope you like chicken sandwiches.'

'Love them. But you needn't have bothered. I'm quite domesticated myself, you know. I took it on myself to provide our lunch.'

'We'll have plenty of choice, then. I have a healthy appetite, don't you?'

'Sure do.' Ric deposited the bag on the back seat, alongside a substantial-looking basket covered with a cloth, and opened the car door for her.

'I thought we'd go up the Thames coast and to Coromandel township, then to Whitianga and back across the peninsula from Tairua to Kopu,' he suggested, handing her a map.

That would give them a round trip taking in the most interesting parts of the peninsula, she agreed.

'You sound very confident with the Maori place-names,' she complimented him. 'My Maori pupils have coached me, but I believe your pronunciation is almost as good as mine, and in such a short time!'

'Dr Simons has been teaching me. It didn't take long to get the hang of pronouncing the vowels, except for that "ai" sound which is almost a long "i" but not quite. And the "wh" which he tells me is neither a "w" nor an "f" sound, but something in between. I'm sure I would horrify him with my attempt at "Whiti-anga".'

'Never mind, a lot of New Zealanders have never mastered the sound of the Maori language, either.'

'Dr Simons tells me there's a move afoot to make the language compulsory in schools,' he commented.

'Yes, there have been moves in that direction. But there's some strong opposition, too.'

'On what grounds?'

'Oh, that there are more important things to learn; that the children will be confused by trying to learn two languages at a young age; that most of them will never use the skill, except to pronounce place names correctly; even, some say, that it's a dying language and it would be pointless to teach them it.'

'It seems a pity for a language to die,' he observed. 'When a language dies, a whole culture goes with it.'

'Mmm, that's exactly why the people who want it taught would like to make it compulsory. They believe that if the language is taught to every child, all New Zealanders will be made aware of the background culture to which it belongs. At the moment, the Maori children learn entirely in English, absorbing the British culture and way of life. They would like to make the process reciprocal.'

'For a comparative newcomer yourself, you seem to know a lot about it,' he commented. 'Where do you get it all from?'

'Other teachers,' she said. 'It's a subject that gets bandied about in staff rooms and at teachers' conferences.'

'Do you have any strong feelings about it?'

'Not strong feelings. But I feel it might be a good idea. This is a multi-racial society. If the teaching of Maori in schools could create greater understanding and harmony between people of different cultural backgrounds, perhaps it would be a good thing.'

They drove up the familiar Thames coast, winding in and out of the numerous small bays as the road followed the contours of the coastline. The sea glimmered blue today, reflecting the sky which was very nearly cloudless. The intense heat of high summer had given way to a pleasant warmth, and the day was almost perfect for driving.

Eventually the road left the coast and began to climb into the hills, until looking back they could see the deep inlets and scattered islands that made this part of the coast resemble Norwegian fjords in their configuration.

Wire fences kept curious sheep and some cattle away from the road as it twisted its way higher into the hills. Later it descended into a grassy valley, and small Maori children waved and smiled at them from farm gateways as they passed.

The small township which had taken the names of the peninsula itself charmed Glenna with its almost Wild West atmosphere fostered by the houses and shops built in the previous century. They explored its main street and bought themselves a cooling drink before carrying on over more winding roads to the other side of the peninsula, with its views of the open sea to the east. At Whitianga, the most popular holiday resort on the peninsula, they stopped for lunch and a swim. Lying on a crescent of white sand at Buffalo Beach, and watching the procession of small boats on the water, they rested after an exhilarating dip in the Pacific.

'Where's that suntan lotion of yours?' Ric asked.

Glenna, lying on her back and enjoying the feel of the sun's warmth on her still damp body, lazily lifted her sunglasses and said, 'Over there, in my bag. You're welcome to use some, if you want.'

'Not for me,' he answered. 'For you.'

'I don't need it,' she said. 'The sun isn't strong, and I've tanned already.'

'Not here, you haven't.' He ran an impudent finger across her body, tracing the top of her swimsuit.

Indignantly she snatched off her glasses and glared at him.

Ric laughed back at her. 'You weren't wearing that swimsuit when you got your tan.'

Involuntarily, she looked down and saw the inch of white skin that showed above her suit. He was right. This was a new one, and it was slightly more daring than the old.

'Here, use it.' Ric handed her the bottle and added, 'I'd hate to see you get burnt.'

'Thank you,' she muttered, obeying him. He watched her and when she had finished, held out his hand for the lotion. 'Want me to do your back?'

'No thanks.'

He grinned and returned the bottle to her bag. Then he leaned on one elbow so that he could see her face. Glenna closed her eyes behind the glasses and ignored him.

She must have dozed, for she woke suddenly to a shower of chilly droplets of water on her bare midriff.

She wriggled, making a sleepy protest. Ric leaned

over her, his shadow blocking the sun, and took off her glasses. His dark eyes were smiling.

'Beast,' she said. 'You did that on purpose, didn't you?'

'No,' he denied. 'But you shouldn't go to sleep in the sun.' He had been in the water again, and his hair was gleaming. He had towelled his chest and arms dry, but water still flattened the dark hair on his tanned legs.

'Why not?' she asked. 'I can think of few things nicer than snoozing in the sun on a beach on a day like this. Anyway, there's nothing else to do but swim.'

'Isn't there?' he quizzed her, and she immediately wished she had not said it. 'Why don't you read your book?' he suggested blandly, and lay back on his towel.

Glenna groped for the sunglasses he had dropped in the sand beside her, and crossly replaced them on her nose.

Ric lay still and apparently utterly relaxed beside her, but Glenna felt restless. Eventually she sat up, gazing at the glittering water with its complement of squealing, laughing swimmers, and the white and occasional red, blue or orange sails that were visible further out to sea.

Warm fingers trailed up her spine and lingered on her shoulder blade.

'You've a little scar there,' Ric's voice said, deep and lazy. 'What happened?'

'I was walking in the bush, and I slipped. The branch that I grabbed broke and sprang back at me, and I sort of fell against it.'

He sat up and pressed his lips to the mark for a long, sweet moment. But when his hands slipped across her shoulders and his head bent to hers, she stiffened.

'*No!*'

He held her for a second longer, looking at her

averted face. Then he said, 'All right—no.'

His arm dropped and he stared out to sea.

'I think I'll have another swim,' Glenna said, to break the tension.

'I'll join you. Then we'd better move on.'

They swam, enjoying the cool salt water and the easing of the slight strain between them. Glenna did not wear a cap, but had plaited her hair and pinned it in a neat coil. There were one or two unexpectedly large breakers, and when she emerged, her hair had lost its neatness. The plait had fallen across her shoulder and was half unravelled.

Ruefully, she undid and combed it out, towelling the ends to stop them dripping. Then she fished in her bag for more pins, and began to re-plait it.

'Why don't you leave it down?' asked Ric. 'It suits you.'

'Thank you,' she said, but her fingers kept on with their deft movements. 'I like it out of the way.'

'Whose way?'

She flicked him a cold glance. 'Mine, of course.' She thrust in some pins and stood up. 'I'll go and change.'

He was back before her, watching her as she crossed the warm sand to his side. Her shirt was as fresh and crisp as ever, and she had freshened up her make-up.

'The spinster schoolmarm to the life,' he said sardonically, surveying her prim neatness.

'Why not?' she asked steadily. 'That's what I am.'

Ric gave a faint snort of derision and took her arm in a rather ungentle hold to guide her across the beach to the car.

At Tairua they stopped for a last look at the sea before turning inland. The beach here sloped steeply, and the breakers were impressive, hurling themselves to shore with foaming urgency. They left the car and watched for a while the ceaseless surge of the ocean almost hypnotic with its power and beauty.

They stopped again several times to appreciate some of the views made available by the road which passed through rugged, bush-clad mountains. Looking across these to the distant sea was a never-to-be-forgotten experience.

The afternoon was drawing to a close as they crossed a bridge spanning a wide, shallow stream, and Ric pulled into a gravelled picnic area on the other side.

'I'm peckish again,' he announced. 'Are there any of those chicken sandwiches left?'

'A few. And some tomato and ham. And some fruit,' Glenna informed him, inspecting the food supply.

They sat at a rustic wooden table with seats attached and satisfied their hunger. Then they investigated a narrow path that led to the stream and found that it was easily crossed by means of the many huge stones that littered its bed. Glenna discarded her shoes to wade in the icy water and pick out stones, worn smooth by the movement of the water.

'Look at the colours!' she said, showing Ric a handful of them. 'When they're dry, they won't be nearly as bright, but even so, there's such a variety.'

There were reds and purples, greens and greys and dappled stones, and a lump of pure white quartz.

'Some people collect them and polish them, you know,' she told Ric. 'Some of these would make lovely jewellery.'

Ric picked out one or two and turned them in his palm. 'They certainly are attractive.' He bent and fished a larger lump of quartz from the water. Running across it was an unmistakable band of gleaming yellow. Disbelievingly, he rubbed his thumb across the golden streak, saying softly, 'Well, I'll be——!'

Glenna laughed at him. 'Fool's gold!' she said.

'Really?'

'Well, I'm no expert, but according to what we were told at the gold camp, from memory I'd say that's what it is. It looks more real than the real thing.'

'Well, I'm keeping it anyway.' He slipped the stone into his pocket. 'Fool or not, I like the look of it.'

They made their way upstream a little way, enjoying the sight of the stream hurrying over and around the vari-coloured boulders and stones that hindered its rush to the sea, and the contrasting greenery of the ferns, lantanas and native trees that lined its mossy banks. The sound of the water blended with the gentle rustling of the wind in the trees and produced an atmosphere of the utmost peace and tranquillity.

They returned hand in hand and in silence to the path down which they had come. As they reached it, Ric pulled her round to face him, within inches of the stream's edge, the trees all round shadowing his face in the gathering dusk.

He held both her hands, and gazed at her upturned face. Then his fingers slid up her arms and softly over her shoulders to frame her face in his hands.

'Don't say no,' he said. And she didn't as he lowered his head and slowly, very gently, kissed her.

It was like returning home after a long, long journey. And Glenna dared not move for fear that the moment would shatter, as so many of her dreams had shattered into wakefulness since they had parted.

But this time, Ric was still there when the kiss ended, holding her hand again, and in silence helping her up the steep path and back to the car.

The drive for the rest of the way was accomplished in almost total silence. Once Glenna remarked on how smoothly the car travelled, and asked who it belonged to.

'I hired it,' he told her. 'For the duration of my stay.' She dried up then, because she didn't want to recall how very temporary his stay was going to be. She smothered the small pain that started, and reminded herself of her determination to enjoy this day and forget all the tomorrows that were to follow.

As they turned down the road to the school, he said, slowing almost to a crawl, 'You wouldn't care to come on to my place—Dr Simons'—for a while?'

She shook her head, not trusting herself to answer, and without comment he completed the turn and picked up speed.

When he stopped in the car park, she said, 'Thank you so much for a wonderful day, Ric.'

'Thank *you*,' he replied. 'Would you care to do it again? Or, perhaps, another dinner?'

'Very well.'

'If we start early, we might go further afield. Would you prefer to travel to Auckland and make a real festive evening?'

'Not if it's a week night, thanks. I have to teach in the mornings, you know.'

'Right, no long trip, then ... that doesn't leave a great deal of choice——'

Hastily she said, 'I don't mind going to the same restaurant again. It was pleasant last time.'

He looked at her rather speculatively. 'Very well. Will Tuesday suit you?'

'Fine.'

As he left her at her door she asked, 'Did you know the trip is on for Thursday? Are you coming?'

'No, I'm afraid not. Having taken today off I'll be too busy this week.' He hesitated, then asked, 'Did Daniel manage to find sufficient helpers?'

'Oh, yes. One of the clubs in Thames is helping.'

'Good.' He touched her cheek lightly with his fingers. 'Goodnight, Glenna.'

*

However, on Monday Glenna was called away from her classroom to take a phone call in Daniel's office.

He indicated the receiver on the desk and went out, leaving the door almost shut, but not quite.

'Glenna?' Ric's voice came over the wire clear and vibrant. 'I'm sorry, I have to cancel our date. Dr Simons wants me in Auckland for a week. We've been invited to meet some people who may be able to help with our tentative plans for the school.'

'Does that mean it won't be closing down?'

'It's too early to say yet, but we hope to avoid that, as you know. I'm not sure if I'll be back at the weekend. I'll catch up with you as soon as I do return.'

'Yes, do that,' she said.

'I have to leave right away,' he went on. 'I'm truly sorry about this.'

'That's all right, I have plenty to keep me busy.'

'And entertained?'

'That too.'

'Glenna—miss me a little.'

He sounded as though he meant it, but she was too wary to reply in kind. 'I'm sure we all will,' she replied calmly.

For a few seconds there was silence. Then he said, 'That wasn't exactly what I meant. See you next week, I hope. Goodbye.'

'Goodbye.'

Daniel came in as she replaced the receiver.

'Finished?' he asked.

'Yes, thank you. Sorry to have kept you out of your office.'

'Don't be silly. Do I dare ask if you enjoyed the outing at the weekend?'

'Very much, thanks. How was yours?'

'Very enjoyable. Hasn't Cleo told you all about it?'

'She hasn't had a chance yet,' said Glenna. 'I daresay we'll hear about it tonight.'

They did, for Cleo was quite excited by her meeting with Charlie Graham and his wife. Over the evening meal, she regaled Peggy and Glenna with details of the day, and her admiration for the man she had met.

'He must be quite old, I suppose,' she said, 'since he was injured during the war.'

'He may be only in his fifties,' Glenna objected mildly, 'if he was in his early twenties during the war. Some were even younger.'

'Well, he looks about forty-five,' said Cleo. 'A big, hearty sort of man with a full beard and a laugh you can hear a mile away. I don't believe I've met anyone who was so very *alive*.'

'And he's been in a wheelchair for over thirty years?' Peggy asked, impressed.

'No, fifteen years.'

'I thought you said he was injured during the war?'

'Yes, but at the time it didn't affect his walking. He was injured by shrapnel, and there were fragments left in his back—his spine. Apparently by an unlucky chance, some—or one—of them shifted years later and led to his legs being paralysed. But he's hardly let it affect his life at all. He just kept on running his business and switched his sporting activities to things that require no legwork, and even took on more work voluntarily to help people he thinks are worse off.'

'You make it sound very darned simple,' Peggy said dryly.

'No, *he* did. I know, Peg, what a hard time he must have had, adjusting and learning to live a normal life when he had to do it in a wheelchair. But he did it. He is *so* normal. I'd love our kids here to meet him, to see what's possible for them.'

'Have you suggested that to Daniel?' Glenna asked. 'I'm sure he wouldn't mind inviting his friend here to meet the children.'

'We have discussed it, yes. Daniel thought it was a good idea, too. He's going to suggest it to Charlie when the trip to the gold camp is over. One thing at a time, he says.'

'What was Charlie's wife like?' Glenna asked.

'*Very* attractive, and so very nice!' said Cleo enthusiastically. 'You know, when Daniel said she had no thought of money when she married Charlie, and how she adored him, I wondered ... I mean, men are such *fools* about women, sometimes, aren't they?'

'Daniel isn't,' Glenna murmured. 'He knows the real gold when he sees it.'

The other two looked at her, and for some reason Cleo blushed.

'Well, anyway,' she went on, 'she's a very nice woman, and they make a lovely couple.'

'Bet you didn't ask Charlie why he married her,' Glenna grinned.

Cleo cast her a withering look. 'I may drop a clanger now and then, but I'm not *that* dim!'

The joke had to be explained to Peggy, of course. Later, when she and Glenna were walking in the dark back to their quarters, Glenna said thoughtfully, 'Do you think Cleo is really fond of Daniel, Peg?'

'Possibly,' Peggy replied casually. 'Under that flippant manner, there's a lot more to Cleo than meets the eye.'

'I know. I think perhaps Daniel is beginning to realise that, too.'

'Do you? Would it bother you?'

'Bother me? Why should it ever bother *me*?'

Peggy began to laugh. 'Well, Cleo thinks there's something going on between you and Daniel.'

'But that's ridiculous! What kind of *something*, may I ask?'

'Well, I assumed she meant a romance. She said she'd come on the two of you, the other night, looking very tense, and she thought you'd been quarrelling. We all know that you and Daniel are probably the least likely members of the staff to quarrel with anyone, let alone each other. And then, she says, you made some cryptic remark about him which implied that you had some sort of secret about him.'

'Oh, really!' Glenna exclaimed. 'Whatever's the matter with Cleo—jumping to conclusions like that! She's quite wrong, you know. There's nothing between Daniel and me like that.'

'I believe you. As for Cleo, I think what is the matter is that she's getting rather fond of our director.'

'Well, I don't see much wrong with that,' Glenna said cheerfully.

CHAPTER ELEVEN

THE goldfield trip was an unqualified success, as Cleo said afterwards. 'Exhausting, nerve-racking—but definitely a success!'

Most of the staff who were not on duty had gathered in the communal lounge, throwing themselves on chairs in various attitudes of comfortable exhaustion. The volunteer helpers had been given a substantial afternoon tea on their return and farewelled with sincere thanks from Daniel and three enthusiastic cheers from the children. Then somehow the children had been occupied with not too exciting activities before they were fed and put to bed. Mrs Newman had served up a hearty meal for the staff, and now they were ready to discuss the day's activity among themselves.

There had been no mishaps, but several staff members recalled heart-stopping moments when over-eager children tried their wheelchairs on too-steep slopes, or attempted to hurry over uneven ground on crutches.

'They all had a wonderful time,' Glenna said. 'They all have their little bottles of gold safely stowed away for the night, labelled with their names.'

'I must write a letter to the bus company,' said Daniel, thinking aloud. 'It was good of them to go to the trouble of removing almost half the seats so that we could get our wheelchairs in.'

'I'll get the children to write some thank you letters too,' said Glenna, 'to the volunteer helpers. We couldn't have done without them, could we?'

There was a chorus of agreement.

'Well——' Glenna stood up, 'after all the excitement, I need to unwind. Anyone going to join me for a brisk walk?'

Several people groaned, and Cleo rolled up her eyes in apparent disbelief. 'You don't mean it? After lugging kids around and bending over a race helping them wash out their gold? I'm aching in every limb! All I want to do is tumble straight into bed.'

'I'll come,' said Daniel. They both looked around the room enquiringly, but no one else was inclined to join them, so to a background of mild insults to their intelligence and mock-admiring comments on their stamina, the two of them went out.

They walked in silence for a time, taking one of the broad smooth paths that wound its way around the quite extensive gardens.

'It's a good way to unwind,' Daniel said as they began to retrace their steps.

'Were you afraid something might have gone wrong today?' Glenna asked. The ultimate responsibility would have been his, she realised.

'Not only that,' he answered.

She glanced at him curiously, but he seemed to be lost in his own thoughts, and she did not want to probe.

He stopped at the door of his quarters and caught her arm as she made to pass on to her own.

'Would you care to come in for a drink, Glenna?'

She hesitated only a moment. 'Thanks. That would round off the day nicely.'

She sat on the sofa while he poured her a sherry.

'I see your carpet came clean,' she commented as he handed her a glass.

'Oh—your little accident.' He sat himself down in a chair opposite her. 'No bother.'

'By the way,' she said, 'I never picked up my clothes.

Every time I've thought of it you haven't been here.'

'I'll get them later. I got them cleaned for you, but I don't think you'll be able to wear them again.'

'Thank you, but you shouldn't have bothered——'

'No bother,' he said again, more firmly this time. He looked down at his glass, swirling the liquid in it. Watching his face, she was aware suddenly that he was looking tense and troubled.

'What's the matter?' she asked quietly.

'Nothing that hasn't been the matter for the last ten years,' he answered. Restlessly, he stood up and wandered over to the small electric fire, glancing at a photograph that stood on the narrow mantel above it. 'My wife died ten years ago today.'

'Oh, Daniel,' Glenna exclaimed softly. 'You must be feeling so——'

'Don't worry,' he said quickly. 'I can cope—I've had a long time to get used to it. I'm sorry, Glenna, I didn't bring you here to burden you with my troubles.'

'You can if you like,' she said. 'You once invited me to burden you with mine, if you remember.'

'An offer which you refused.'

'I may yet need to take you up on it.'

'All right. I'm available if you need me.' He sipped his drink and his eyes returned to the picture on the mantel.

'That's your wife?' Glenna asked.

'Yes.' He stared at it for a while, then said, 'She was——'

'Yes?'

'A super girl. The first time I saw her——' He broke off.

'Please!' Glenna said softly. 'I'd like to hear about her if it doesn't hurt you too much.'

'You mean,' he said, smiling wryly, 'that you're willing to be used as a wailing wall if I want to talk.'

'You said once that I'd been using you, in a rather different way.'

'True, but I made you pay for it, didn't I? And that was only a means of taking out my own frustrations on you.'

'What does that mean?'

'Oh—a lot of things.' He settled lower in his chair and ran a finger round the rim of his glass. 'The truth is, *I* was the one who was jealous.'

She looked startled, and he smiled. 'It's all right, I'm not about to declare my undying passion for you. You wouldn't welcome it if I did, would you?'

'I'd be—very flattered,' she managed to say. 'But——'

'*But* you're in love with Ric Burnett.'

'That was a long time ago, Daniel——'

'That was last Tuesday, in my office,' he interrupted ruthlessly. 'I saw the look on your face when you heard his voice on the phone.'

'Well,' she said inadequately, 'I'm not talking about it, if you don't mind. You won't say anything to Ric will you?'

He raised an eyebrow reproachfully, and she muttered, 'Sorry.'

'Anyway,' he went on, 'when I said I was jealous, I meant in a general way. You started it, the morning I patched you up here. I gave you some well-meant advice, remember?'

'About not pining for a man who didn't want me?'

'Yes—and something about other fish in the sea.'

'Men in the world,' she murmured.

'Same thing,' he grinned, and she smiled back. 'I'd just kissed you, if you remember.' He watched her eyes duck away from his and then determinedly return, and his grin grew slightly. Her own mouth curved up wryly. 'It occurred to me that I might take my own advice. I'd never thought of marrying again, but that morning for the first time, the thought crossed my mind.'

'But not with *me* in mind.'

'Not exactly. But you were an obvious—candidate. I'm sorry if this sounds cold-blooded. What I mean is that I've begun to look at the women I know in a different light. I'm putting this very badly, I'm afraid. It's not that I'm ticking off possibilities.'

'I know,' Glenna said calmly. 'You've simply stopped thinking of yourself as a married man.'

He cast her a grateful look. 'Thank you, Glenna. That's exactly what I mean. Anyway, when I realised that you still care for Ric, I was sorry for myself, because it wasn't me. Because there's no one who cares for me that way.' He sighed. 'Am I making sense?'

'Very much so. And let me tell you, there are plenty of nice young women who'll be awfully pleased if you've really stopped being a married man.'

He looked both pleased and embarrassed—so much that Glenna laughed and changed the subject.

She accepted another glass of wine, and then a third, because their conversation was interesting and it was cosy and restful in the small room, and because Daniel wanted her company. Eventually she found herself telling him about how she had met Ric, and what had happened to them eight years ago. He listened sympathetically and with very little comment, and she wept just a little, giving a watery little laugh afterwards. 'I think I've had a little too much of your lovely sherry, you know. I'm getting to the maudlin stage!'

He made her a cup of coffee then, and she left afterwards, taking the bundle of clean clothing that he put in her arms, and swinging the cleaned shoes from her hand. She dropped one of them and giggled, and Daniel gave a mock sigh and picked it up and escorted her to her door.

'Thank you,' she said, taking the shoe from him.

'And thanks for getting these cleaned. I must leave my clothes in your flat more often. The tear might mend if I can match the wool,' she added thoughtfully.

'Glenna!' he exclaimed in pretended alarm. 'Please, have a care for my reputation.' He nodded and waved in the direction of another staff member who was passing by and looking a little curiously at them in the dimness.

Glenna laughed. Everyone knew both of them, and she was sure that no one would put any but the most innocent construction on their conversation, even if it was overheard.

Ric arrived at the school with Dr Simons at the weekend, but not until Sunday afternoon. They were closeted with Daniel until dinner time, and didn't stay for the meal. Glenna had only glimpsed them in the distance, and she experienced an acute sense of depression mixed with a little annoyed anger, when Daniel came into the dining room alone.

Next day, however, she looked up during a lesson to see Ric hovering in the doorway of her classroom.

The children looked interested as she hurried towards him. He stepped back and she walked into the passageway with him.

'I'm sorry about yesterday,' he said. 'Dr Simons wanted to get away, since he travelled back to Auckland last night. And I didn't think you would thank me for making you conspicuous in the dining room.'

'It's all right,' she smiled.

'Are you free tonight?'

She was free every night of the week, but she was not going to tell him that. 'Yes,' she said coolly, and accepted his invitation to dinner, briefly assented to the time he suggested, and slipped back into her classroom quickly.

He was punctual, and so was she. She met him at the door, dressed in a pale blue silk shirt and darker blue skirt.

'Blue suits you,' he said as though he meant it. His eyes flicked to her hair, in its usual knot, but he made no comment on that.

'I've discovered there's a music recital on tonight,' he told her in the car. 'Would you care to hear it, after dinner?'

She said she would, and they dined in the same restaurant as before and then went on to a small hall to hear classical music played to an appreciative audience who were all too willing to put up with hard chairs and poor acoustics in the interests of a rare cultural treat.

'I'm afraid conditions were a little primitive,' Ric apologised afterwards.

'I don't mind. I enjoyed the music.'

'You always had impeccable manners, Glenna,' he said rather mockingly.

'No, I mean it!' she protested vehemently. 'I've had a thoroughly enjoyable evening. I loved it.'

His face softened. 'Does that include the company?'

She gave him a sideways look and didn't answer.

She heard him laugh softly as he opened the door of the car for her. He slid into his seat and asked, 'Straight home?'

'Straight home, please,' she answered firmly.

But when he took her to the door of the flat she relented and offered him coffee.

He sat on the sofa, and she gave him his cup and took one of the two easy chairs for herself.

'Am I allowed to ask how the negotiations went last week?' she asked.

He smiled. 'Ulterior motives, Glenna?' When she looked blank, he explained. 'Did you invite me in so that you could pump me about future plans for the school?'

'No, of course not. But naturally I'm interested. We all would like to know how you think things will go at the board meeting. Are you going to recommend the school be closed?'

He stirred his coffee thoughtfully. 'I hope not. But I expect to recommend some changes. The aspects that I've been asked to investigate are financial and administrative, of course, but you may find that while the board is reassessing, it will take other factors into account as well.'

'Other factors? Like its isolation?'

He glanced at her sharply. 'Someone's been talking to you.'

'Daniel,' she said absently, missing the expression in his eyes. 'He says we're too cut off from the community here. It *is* a problem. Even some of the parents find it difficult to visit their children. But the only way to solve that would be to move the whole school, and surely the board can't afford that?'

'I can't really tell you anything,' he said abruptly. 'I have a brief to report to the board, and it's hardly ethical to discuss it with the staff beforehand. Perhaps Daniel will tell you more.'

'Yes, I see.' Glenna was a little hurt by his change of tone. 'I'm sorry if I spoke out of turn.' She put down her cup, and asked, 'When will your report be ready?'

'A couple of weeks should do it.' Ric too placed his cup on the low table. She stared at the two empty cups, side by side, thinking that two weeks was a very short time.

'Will you—be going home after that?'

'I'll probably take a week off to have a real holiday. I've seen very little of New Zealand, and I'm told there are things I ought to see.'

'Oh, yes.' She wasn't going to let him see how much it mattered that after two weeks from now she might never see him again. 'Boiling pools at Rotorua, limestone caves and glow-worms at Waitomo, fishing at Taupo. *Do* you fish?'

'No, but perhaps I'll try my hand. Have *you* seen all those?'

'I don't fish either, but the glow-worm caves, and Rotorua, yes.'

'With Daniel?'

'No,' she said blankly. 'I didn't know Daniel then.'

'How long have you known him?'

'Two years. Since I've been here at the school.'

'You seem fond of him.'

'I am.' She was groping, wondering if his casual tone was a cover for something else. 'He's a friend as well as my boss,' she said.

'Just good friends?' he murmured. And before she could answer that, he said idly, 'I daresay you've had a good many men friends since I knew you.'

'Some,' she said cautiously.

His eyes flicked over her with a glance that made her slightly uneasy. Had he slightly emphasised that word 'friends'? 'Does Daniel object to my seeing you?'

'Not in the least. He wouldn't dream of interfering in my friendships. It's none of his business. We're not living in Victorian times now, after all,' she added, thinking of the teachers and servants and even clerks of former times whose lives had been run by their employers, even in the private sphere.

'No, we're not, indeed!' Ric drawled, his narrowed eyes unreadable.

Glenna got up and took the cups into her tiny kitchen, hoping he would take the hint and go. When she came back into the room, he was standing.

'Thanks for the meal, and the concert,' she said.

His eyes looked amused. He moved towards the door, saying, 'We'll do it again, shall we?'

'I'd like that.'

He put out his hand, and she hesitated a moment and then placed hers in it. 'Goodnight,' she said.

'Is that the best you can do?' He dropped her hand and caught at her shoulders. 'Try again.'

Her mouth accepted his kiss, but her body was tense in his arms, because she was afraid of betraying herself with the honesty of her response, if she relaxed.

'What's the matter?' he muttered, lifting his head a fraction, and running his hand down her spine. She gave an infinitesimal shake of her head in reply, and he frowned and lowered his lips to hers, more passionately than before, as if determined to win a real response from her.

It was useless. She went more rigid and then began to fight him.

He let her go and she turned away.

'No again?' he said quietly.

She nodded without speaking, and heard him open and close the door as he went out.

It was possible to make a day-trip to Rotorua. When Ric suggested it, Glenna was glad to accept. She wanted a chance to wipe out the memory of that last evening—or at least its ending, that had been, obviously, unsatisfactory for him, and unsettling for her.

Not, she thought, that a whole day in his company was very likely to be conducive to peace of mind, when she was already counting the days to his departure.

They left early and arrived in the small city of Rotorua at eleven in the morning. The smell of sulphur was all-pervading, and steam rose from all kinds of unexpected places—backyards, small cairns of stones by the roadside that protected the unwary from stepping into the hot springs beneath them, and the edges of the lake where they strolled after lunch.

They explored cautiously the eerie delights of Whakarewarewa, with its mud pools boiling mysteriously like enormous pots of porridge, its hot and cold streams running side by side, and its spectacular geyser, which obligingly shot a twenty-foot-high jet of boiling water and steam into the air for them from a gaping, irregular fissure in the sulphur-coated earth.

Later, they looked around a model Maori village, admiring the intricate whorls and grooves of the carvings which represented in grotesque form the human and animal beings of Maori myth and history. At Ohinemutu, on the outskirts of Rotorua, they saw a tiny church lined with carefully executed interwoven reed and flax work in criss-cross patterns, and featuring the unique sandblasted window decoration of 'Christ walking on the water.' The figure, wearing a Maori cloak, was superimposed on the view outside of the lake, and sitting in the front pew they could see how it had been made to give the impression that the Christ was indeed walking on the waters of Lake Rotorua.

Throughout the day, Glenna was conscious of the touch of Ric's hand as he held hers while they negotiated uneven pathways, or held her arm firmly as they crossed a road, and of the quality of his smile, intimate and tender when he looked at her. She was conscious that all day he was gently, subtly, and with no hint of importunity or passion, making love to her.

It was dark when they reached Thames, and he sped right past the turning to the school.

Glenna turned her head quickly, and he said, easily, 'Surprise. I've prepared dinner for us—I told you I was domesticated.'

He made it very difficult to refuse. If she made an

issue of it, she was going to look both churlish and a prude.

Ric made her sit down while he finished off the dinner, and when it came, forty minutes later, it was indeed delicious. A soup followed by chicken which was pre-cooked and then coated in crumbs on his return, and fried in butter, served with salad and french-fried potatoes. And for afters, cheese and crackers and a bowl of oranges, bananas and crisp red apples to choose from.

'That was lovely!' she complimented him as he passed her a cup of coffee afterwards. 'You weren't kidding when you said you were domesticated, were you?'

He smiled and sipped his coffee. 'Have you enjoyed yourself today?'

'Very much. What about you? You're the tourist.'

'Is that what I am?' He eyed her. 'I suppose you don't look on yourself as a visitor any more.'

'Not really.' She sipped her coffee and lapsed into silence.

He finished his, and stood to take her empty cup, putting it on the table with his own. When he turned, looking at her sitting in the upholstered, high-backed chair. 'Relax,' he said. 'That's the most comfortable chair in the room, and you look as stiff as a poker.'

'It's my hair,' she confessed. The heavy knot of it on her neck was getting in the way as she attempted to lean her head back.

'Take it down,' he said indifferently. 'Or sit on the sofa.' He strolled over to stand in front of her, and said softly, 'Or better still, both.'

He bent and took her hands and pulled her up. Unheeding of her not very determined resistance, he pushed her over to the sofa and sat beside her. Glenna turned to him to protest, and saw the smile in his eyes as he raised his hands and began pulling out pins and dropping them carelessly on the floor. She raised her own hands to stop him, saying feebly, 'There's no need now.'

'There is.' His fingers felt the elastic band that held the beginning of the knot, and gently tugged it off. She tried to stop him, and caught at his wrist, but he took one of her hands and brought it forward to his chest, and simply ignored the other as his hand slipped to the back of her neck, entangled now in her hair.

'No,' she said feebly, as he said, 'Yes,' and it was already too late, because he was kissing her and his lips were firm and gentle. She stopped holding his wrist and let her hand slip on to his shoulder and then to the back of his neck, and when he let go her other hand to pull her closer and stroke her back, she moved it of her own free will against his chest, loving the feel of its hard warmth beneath his shirt.

He moved so that her head was pressed into the curve of his shoulder, and his mouth insisted on the kind of ready response she had given him years before. She gave it unstintingly, and felt her own passion increase with the tempo of his. She felt him flick open the buttons of his shirt so that her exploring hand could slip inside it, and she wanted that—to feel his skin, slightly fuzzed with hair, warm under her fingers.

His mouth left hers and pressed against her throat, and she sighed with pleasure. He tugged her blouse from the waistband of her skirt, and returned his lips to hers, but some warning bell was niggling in her brain. With anyone else, she would have stopped this long before. While her body was urging her to fulfilment, her common sense was crying feebly to be heard. Some part of her wanted to cry stop, and gain some time to make decisions that were not clouded by the mists of love and passion.

Ric must have felt some hint of her hesitation, because his hand hardened on the smoothness of her back, and he raised his head, and said urgently, his voice thick and low, '*Please*, Glenna. Give me something to remember when I go.'

Cold water could not have been more effective.

She fought herself blindly from his suddenly angry embrace, and got herself across the room to the window. She looked out at the sea, but it might have been anything at all. She stood with her arms folded about herself, rigid with shame and unshed tears.

CHAPTER TWELVE

THE silence behind her was profound. Minutes ticked away.

Then Ric spoke, very low, very clear. Very hard.

'Would you mind telling me why? You obviously don't find me repulsive.'

'I'm sorry, I didn't mean to——' She tried again. 'I shouldn't have let you——'

'Then why did you?'

'I did say no.'

'Yes, but not as though you meant it.'

'I didn't realise how far——'

'—I meant to go?' His tight, angry control broke. 'For heaven's sake, Glenna! You're not a nineteen-year-old virgin now!'

'No,' she said, and her breath caught in a slight, hysterical little laugh with more than a hint of bitterness. 'I'm a twenty-seven-year-old one.'

She heard him draw in a quick breath that sounded as though he was about to say something violent. Then, seconds later, he said, 'I happen to know that's not true.'

The shock of that brought her swinging round to face him, eyes wide and dark with shock and anger. 'What on *earth* do you mean by that?'

Ric was on his feet, and there was both anger and contempt in his face. Glenna shivered inside, because she had never seen him in quite such a temper before, and the contempt was new and shattering.

'You ought to be a bit more discreet when you visit your lovers,' he sneered.

'What are you talking about? I don't have lovers—I don't even have *one* lover.'

'Oh, yes, I forgot. "Just good friends" is the euphemism, these days, isn't it?'

It must be a nightmare, Glenna told herself. This couldn't possibly be happening in real life. 'Just good friends'? She had heard him say something like that before . . .

Comprehension, of a sort, began to dawn in her face.

'*Daniel?*' she said, disbelief making her voice unsteady.

'I saw you leaving his flat the very first night I was here—or rather, in the morning. Almost in broad daylight, in fact. But you were wearing the same clothes you'd been wearing the night before, at dinner. It's the only time I've seen you with your hair down, until now. You looked deliciously dishevelled, not at all like a schoolmarm. Daniel seemed suitably grateful for your —friendship.'

If he had been standing closer she would have slapped the horrible, contemptuous smile from his face. She was trembling with anger, more furious than she had ever been in her life.

'What a *disgusting* mind you have!' she said. 'There was nothing to be discreet about, as anyone at the school except *you* would have known. If you'd bothered to come out of whatever corner you were skulking in when you were spying on us, we might have explained——'

'I never skulk,' he interrupted coldly. 'I happen to be an early riser. Dr Simons and I were sleeping in the hospital wing across the courtyard. I simply looked out of the window and saw you.'

'And jumped to conclusions,' she said bitterly.

'Daniel happens to be a doctor. I fell and hurt myself, and he took me into his flat to treat me.'

She was about to say, *You saw the scar*, but he spoke again. 'Kissing it better, was he? *All night?*'

Suddenly her anger left her, and she felt sick and shaken. It was useless to try and convince him. He had believed this of her ever since he had come here. He must have seen Daniel's innocent, impulsive kiss, and that was something this hard, jeering man would never understand in a million years.

'I don't have to explain anything to you,' she said. 'Would you mind taking me home? If there was another way of getting there, believe me, I'd use it.'

Ric drove with controlled care along the winding road, and Glenna sat beside him, rigidly calm, but weeping all the way inside. *Like the little pig*, she thought, *all the way home*, and clamped her lips tightly to suppress an hysterical giggle. If she started that, Ric would probably slap her, and that would be the last straw.

She tried to make her mind a blank, but it was too hard altogether. She kept recalling incidents, phrases, that had cropped up at different times and that all took on a new and humiliating significance in the light of what had taken place tonight. She had been at such pains to assure him that Daniel was only a friend, that there was nothing serious between them. All it had meant to Ric was that she was sleeping with a man in whom she was only mildly interested, that friendship was enough for her to indulge in the most intimate relationship with a man. And if she was 'available' to one, why not to another? Why should she not give Ric 'something to remember' when he had gone? All his tender glances and his warm laughter, the sweet wooing, had been leading to nothing more than a one night stand, a sordid little episode to cap his New Zealand holiday.

She stumbled out of the car even before he pulled at the handbrake, telling him she didn't want him to come with her. She walked quickly to her door, and heard the car roar out of the car park before she had managed, with shaking fingers, to fit her key into the lock.

Somehow she got through the following day. The children, always sensitive to mood, were fractious and Glenna knew she was not teaching well. By the end of the day she had almost reached screaming point.

She had seen Ric once or twice in the distance, and had gone to her flat at lunchtime and boiled herself an egg rather than risk meeting him in the dining room, in case he stayed for lunch. She knew it would be impossible to avoid him for ever, but the wounds were too new and raw to stand the salt of his nearness just now.

His car was gone after school, and she breathed more freely. She went to the dining room as usual although she had no appetite, not wanting to cause comment or have her friends fussing round her.

Cleo, though, commented on her wan appearance.

'The children have been little fiends today,' she said in answer to Cleo's concern, stifling her conscience, which told her that if the children were difficult it had been because she was less than her usual efficient self. 'As a matter of fact,' she said with perfect truth, 'I have a headache. I'll turn in early tonight, I think.'

'Sounds like a good idea. Do you have something you can take?'

'Aspirin usually does the trick.'

She took two aspirins and had a bath and put on

a warm violet robe that her family had sent her last
Christmas. She shook out her hair and was sitting on
the sofa brushing it and watching a TV programme on
her small set, hoping it would relax her and put her in
the mood for sleep, when someone knocked at the door.

She had never had visitors at night except Peggy or
Cleo dropping in for a chatter. This would be Cleo,
come to see if she was all right.

She called 'Come in!' and twisted round, brush in
hand, to greet her friend.

When she saw who it was, she uncurled her legs from
under her and stood up in one desperate, furious movement.

'*Get out!*' she breathed.

'You just said, "Come in",' said Ric, closing the door
with a decisive click behind him, and walking into the
room.

'I was expecting it to be Cleo, not *you*. Nor one of
my legion of lovers,' she added.

She could have sworn he flinched.

'You said you don't have a legion of lovers,' he said
quietly. 'Nor even one.'

'That's right. But you don't believe me.'

'I do. I've come to apologise. On my knees, if you
like.'

But last night he had been so adamant. And she had
refused to explain fully, after he had patently dis-
believed the main detail.

'Oh, I see,' she said finally. 'Daniel's story tallies with
mine, I suppose. Didn't occur to you I might have
spent the rest of last night with him, and coached him
in what to say?'

'I haven't spoken to Daniel about it. Your word is
good enough for me.'

'It wasn't enough last night.'

'Last night I was totally unreasonable.'

'I noticed.'

'There was a reason,' he said. 'Sexual frustration is apt to warp a man's judgment for a time.'

'I suppose so,' she said vaguely, lifting the hairbrush in her hand and inspecting it for no particular reason. When she lifted her eyes again to his, his lips were twitching into a smile.

'Oh, my darling!' he said, causing a very peculiar sensation in the region of her heart. 'If anything was needed to convince me of your total innocence, that remark would have done it.'

Uncertainly, she smiled back at him. 'I don't see why. Don't you want to know the whole story?'

'No.'

That was clear enough, but when she looked at the thing dispassionately, she could well understand the conclusions he had jumped to.

'I suppose,' she said, 'in this day and age, it's rather silly to expect people not to make certain assumptions on evidence like that.'

'In this day and age, people who make such assumptions would certainly not be thought to have *disgusting* minds,' he said. 'Except possibly by perfectly innocent parties.'

'Was that what convinced you?'

'I told you, your word is good enough.'

'Thank you.'

'Do you know that gown, and this light, make your eyes look violet?' he added.

'No. Would you like some coffee?' The sudden change of subject had her completely confused.

He smiled with real amusement, and said, 'Am I keeping you up?'

'No, I had a headache, but it's gone. I took some aspirin.' She went to the kitchen and began making coffee and trying to sort her thoughts.

He was sitting in an armchair, looking at the abstract on the wall. He hardly glanced at her as he took the coffee cup from her, and returned to studying the painting.

Glenna returned to her seat on the sofa, tucking up her legs as before. 'Could you live with it now, do you think?' she asked him.

He turned his eyes to her. 'Yes. Yes, I think it could grow on me,' he said.

Could I? she wanted to say. Instead, she asked, 'Is the coffee all right?'

'Fine.'

For no reason, except that for once she felt at ease with him, because he seemed relaxed himself, she smiled at him.

His mouth moved slightly in answer to it, but she noticed now that he was not so much relaxed as utterly wary. There were signs of strain about his mouth, and his eyes looked tired. He had sunk into the chair as though he never wanted to leave it. He finished his coffee but went on cradling the cup in his hands, as though it was too much of an effort to lean forward and deposit it on the table.

'You ought to be in bed,' she said.

Ric smiled slightly, his eyes for an instant kindling into teasing warmth. 'Is that an offer?'

'No.' But her lips curved in acknowledgment of the gentle jibe.

'No,' he repeated, sighing, and closing his eyes as he linked his hands behind his head, 'I didn't think it was.'

'Are you going to sleep?' she asked, amused. He looked younger with his eyes closed. She remembered the hours she had spent by his bed at the hospital, holding his hand while he slept.

'Would it bother you if I did?' he asked lazily. And without giving her a chance to answer he went on,

'But of course it would. I might not wake for hours and your reputation would be ruined.'

'I'm not worried about my reputation,' she said.

'What, then?'

My self-control, she thought. She got up and took the cup off his lap. 'Sleep if you want to,' she said softly. 'Have the sofa, if you like.'

Ric opened his eyes and looked up at her. His eyes were very dark and there was gentleness in them, and a kind of sadness.

'You trust me?' he said.

'Yes.'

He got up and took the cup from her hand and laid it on the table. Then he put his hands on her wool-clad shoulders, so gently he was barely touching her. 'The trouble is,' he said, 'I don't trust myself.'

That makes two of us, she thought.

'Will you tell me something?' he asked. 'Why have you always said no?'

'To you?'

'To everyone.'

'Several reasons,' she said. 'But mostly, I suppose, because for me, total intimacy goes with total commitment.'

The sadness in his eyes had deepened into pain. She felt the hands on her shoulders tighten.

'I can't offer you commitment.'

'I know,' she whispered. He had never loved her enough for that, though he had always cared for her, a little. 'And I can't offer you anything less.'

He bent his head and kissed her with the utmost tenderness, and she felt moisture on her cheeks and thought with mild surprise, *I'm* crying. Then he was cradling her head against his shoulder for just an instant, his face pressed into her hair.

She felt cold when he abruptly released her. She was

still standing there when his voice reached her from
the doorway before he closed it behind him. It was
almost a whisper, and not a very steady one at that.
'Goodbye, sweet.'

Glenna found she was beyond tears. The enormity of
a fate which had offered her a second chance and a
second heartbreak was overwhelming.

But as before, she found that habit was at least
a substitute for living. Ric was rarely seen at the school
that week, for which she was thankful. Daniel said
that his investigation was almost finished, and he believed the other man was at last getting some real
leisure.

Cleo expressed some concern over Glenna's depression even though Glenna had made an enormous effort
to hide it. And Daniel was not fooled either. Both they
and Peggy were unobtrusively helpful, and she was
grateful for their tactful understanding, and their restraint. They asked no questions.

Charlie Graham and his wife Susan came and stayed
for three days. They arrived on Friday, and Charlie
spoke to the children during school time, about his
work and his recent trip overseas to compete inter-
nationally with other disabled sportsmen. The children
listened, fascinated. He showed slides of the sights he
had seen in other countries, and fired them with a
desire to do the same when they were old enough.

On Saturday, he showed some of them how to use a
bow and arrow and throw a javelin. They gathered
round his burly figure with great enthusiasm, and
even when he was simply propelling himself around the
grounds, exploring the surroundings with his custom-
ary energy, the children eagerly greeted him as he
passed or even followed him. And he would slow his
chair so that they were able to keep up.

Even Glenna was able to feel some enthusiasm. 'He's very patient,' she commented to Susan as they sat together, watching Charlie telling some story which involved a lot of gestures, and eliciting shouts of delighted laughter from the group of children he was entertaining. 'And he's so good for them.'

'Charlie's good for everybody,' his wife replied with quiet pride. She was a serenely beautiful woman, dark-haired but with strands of silver beginning to show. Glenna could imagine her with it snowy white in old age, framing her face with its faintly aristocratic nose and deep-set brown eyes.

'Had you known him long, before you married?' Glenna asked.

'Do you mean, was he disabled when I married him?' Susan asked dryly.

'No, I already knew that,' replied Glenna calmly.

'I beg your pardon,' the other woman said sincerely. 'I'm afraid I've become over-sensitive. I should have known you weren't just being nosey. You're not the type, are you?'

'I hope not,' Glenna smiled.

'I had known Charlie years ago,' Susan told her. 'He was a friend of my husband—I was married before. We lost touch, and after my first husband died, we met again—actually, at the funeral. Charlie was such a tower of strength, I'm afraid I leaned on him quite shamelessly for a time. You see, my husband had been ill for a long time, and nursing him had rather taken it out of me. I had to be strong, for him, and in a way it was a great relief to be able to let go.'

'I can imagine he would be very comforting to lean on.'

'Yes, and the funny thing is, he didn't seem to realise it. He was very peculiar about marrying me.' She laughed at the expression on Glenna's face. 'I'm sorry,

I'm embarrassing you with my confidences. I'm not usually so garrulous.'

'No, please!' Glenna exclaimed. 'I'm not embarrassed at all. I was only dying to ask you what you meant by "peculiar" and I didn't like to ask.'

'What a nice young woman you are! I do believe you're like Charlie, someone people like me can lean on. Daniel has that quality too. It's a sort of inner strength some people have.'

Privately, Glenna was sure that Susan Graham had a good deal of inner strength of her own, but she quietly accepted the compliment and waited for the other woman to continue her story.

'I knew Charlie liked me,' she continued. 'But he ignored every hint I gave him, and when in desperation I told him I'd like to marry him, he said he wasn't in need of a nurse, thank you, and if I wanted to marry again I ought to choose someone who would look after *me*, not the other way round. I said that was exactly what I *was* doing, of course, which rather took the wind out of his sails.'

Glenna chuckled. 'And then he proposed?'

'Accepted my proposal, you mean. Not immediately. He was very suspicious for a while, but after a good deal of argument I finally convinced him that I didn't simply fancy myself in the role of Florence Nightingale —My dear, what *is* the matter?'

For Glenna, reminded of a similar accusation hurled at herself once, long ago, had flinched and suddenly turned pale.

'Nothing,' she said with some effort. 'Really. I—a bit of a headache. It just throbbed, that's all.'

'And here I am nattering at you and keeping you in this hot sun! My dear, do go and lie down.'

Glenna did go, but not to lie down. She busied herself in her classroom until Daniel came looking for her.

'You're going to need some glad-rags tonight,' he told her. 'You're going out to dinner.'

'I am?'

'Dr Simons wants you, the Grahams, Cleo and myself, to join him and Ric.'

'I'm not going!' she said quickly, emphatically.

'Yes, you are, and that's an order. No member of my staff is going to snub the chairman of the board.'

It was so unlike him to pull rank that Glenna stared open-mouthed, for a moment. Then she tried again, desperately. 'Daniel, please—you don't understand. And anyway, I have a headache——'

'Take some aspirin. If that doesn't work, I'll fix you up with something stronger.' He leaned over the desk and stroked his thumb over her averted cheek. 'It'll be all right, Glenna. Trust me.'

It was not as bad as she expected. Ric gave her a tight smile and turned back to helping Dr Simons dispense drinks, and then hardly glanced at her again all evening.

Daniel and Cleo sat with her on the sofa while they had pre-dinner drinks, and she was relieved to find herself placed at the table between Charlie and Daniel, with Ric opposite her, flanked by Cleo and Susan, and Dr Simons at the head of the table.

Glenna was not able to avoid looking at him altogether, but only once their eyes clashed and held, his quite blank, until she dragged her gaze away and passed some banal remark to Charlie, on her right.

When they were all replete, though Glenna could not have told anyone what she had eaten, Dr Simons produced a bottle of champagne, and solemnly filling glasses for all of them, proposed a toast.

'To the future of the Helen Duke Memorial School.'

Cleo put Glenna's thoughts into words. 'You mean it

will continue, Dr Simons?'

'It appears so, my dear,' he told her. 'The board has to give its approval yet, but Ric, and Daniel and I have, we think, worked out a viable plan for the future of the school. And our friend Charlie here also has a finger in the pie.'

When the toast had been drunk, Cleo demanded explanations. Ric, Daniel and Dr Simons laughed and obliged. The details were not able to be divulged until the board had met, and the women were warned not to talk about the plan to anyone as yet, but it involved the sale of the present buildings and grounds of the school, and the purchase of another site, in less isolated surroundings, close to ordinary schools where the children would be able to attend. Extra finance would be made available at very low interest by Ric's firm, Charlie, and a small group of other businessmen who were willing to help. Some would go towards building a new school, which could be smaller since full-time schooling was not going to be a major part of its work, but would have the advantage of being specially built for the disabled, instead of converted from an ordinary building. The bulk of the rest would be invested to provide an income for the running of the school.

'How did Charlie get involved in this?' Glenna asked Daniel quietly, later. He was sitting beside her again, on the sofa, having seen to it that Charlie was comfortably placed and talking to Ric.

'I sounded him out that day that Cleo and I went to visit him. Ric had told me what direction his ideas were taking, and we needed some fairly well-off people who were prepared to invest their money in a charity. Charlie is the only one I know,' he grinned. 'But he knows a few more, and he's adept at arm-twisting.'

'Did you know your husband was going to contribute?' Glenna asked, turning to Susan Graham.

'Yes, and I heartily approve. Money has helped us, why shouldn't we use some of it to help others? It's true that money can't buy health or happiness,' she went on, 'but it does make ill-health or unhappiness easier to bear, if it's used the right way.'

Ric had to drive them home, because when Daniel tried to start his car, the motor was utterly dead. After several futile minutes, it was obvious the car was not going to start. Charlie's collapsible chair was transferred from the boot of Daniel's car to Ric's, and Charlie moved by Dr Simons and Daniel to the front seat, as Ric manoeuvred the chair in and closed the boot.

It was a big car, and Susan was able to slide in beside her husband, while Daniel and the two girls occupied the rear seat.

They were approaching one of the bends when the headlights came at them, much too fast around the corner ahead, and the other driver, who had been travelling in the centre of the narrow road, pulled too far to the left to over-compensate, and drove off the edge to land with sickening suddenness on the sand and rocks ten feet below. The nose hit the beach first, and there was horrible grace in the way the car flipped up and turned itself right over.

Ric stopped with the bonnet almost touching the cliff on the other side of the road, as far off the tarseal as he could. Then they were all, except Charlie, who was swearing in a low and steady stream of words, out and running across the road, scrambling down on to the sand.

There were rocks that had prevented the car from landing completely on its roof. One man had crawled out, bleeding and with a useless leg. Daniel leaned into a smashed window and turned off the ignition before checking the man quickly by the light of the torch Ric carried, and gave Cleo some quick instructions.

There was someone else. 'He's alive,' Daniel said. 'He was thrown out and then the car landed on top of him.'

Cleo had opened a first-aid box that Ric had handed her and was attending to the first man, with Susan's help.

'We could probably lift it off,' said Ric.

'Don't be a fool!' Daniel snapped.

'I'm willing to give it a try.'

'As a doctor I'm not willing to let you! And if you attempt it I'll not help. I've left my bag in the boot of my car. Will you get back in yours and fetch it for me, please, at the double. We're not far from Dr Simons. It would be quicker to phone an ambulance from there rather than try houses on the way, which may be unoccupied or not have a phone. See to it, please.'

Ric hesitated a moment longer, and Daniel said, '*Dammit*, man, will you get going!'

He left the torch, and sprinted back to the car.

Daniel was looking round the beach, saying as he picked up a long piece of driftwood, and shoved it under the car, next to one of the rocks, 'Glenna, go back to the road and flag down the next car that comes. Tell them I need help, if there are any able-bodied men in it. Otherwise tell them to get the hell out of the way.'

She was lucky. A car load of brawny teenagers stopped for her frantic waving, and were only too willing to help. Daniel, giving up his attempt to lever it up with the bit of wood, accepted their help to heave the car over on to its wheels. A muted cheer was quickly stilled as they caught sight of the man they had freed.

Glenna closed her eyes while she held the torch for

Daniel and Cleo, and was profoundly thankful when Ric returned with Daniel's bag, and relieved her.

Next morning it seemed like a dream that she had had in the night. Daniel had insisted on giving her a pill. She had been too shocked and tired to think last night, but sleep had sharpened her mind. She dressed quickly and brushed out her hair, then went out to waylay Daniel when she saw him crossing the grounds.

'Why wouldn't you let Ric try to lift that car?' she demanded without preamble.

'Two men couldn't have done it,' he answered.

'There were three perfectly healthy women there too. And I know you're not silly enough to think that women are too delicate to help.'

'They're not as strong as men.'

'Then why not send me to get your bag, and let Ric help lift the car? You were protecting him, weren't you?'

'All right—Ric had a back injury once. I didn't want to risk aggravating it again.'

'He's supposed to be completely cured.'

'Is that what he——' Daniel stopped. 'It still troubles him at times—old injuries sometimes do. I prescribed some pain relief for him when he ran out of supplies. And that makes him my patient, Glenna. I can't discuss this with you.'

'Okay, let's discuss a hypothetical case, a case similar to Charlie's. There were fragments of shrapnel in Charlie's back that shifted and paralysed him years later. Could that happen to someone who was injured in a fire accident who had metal fragments in his spine?'

'Glenna——'

'*Could it?*' she asked fiercely.

'Yes. And excessive strain on his back is—could be

dangerous, in your hypothetical case. Even without that——'

'The *fool*!' Glenna exclaimed with some intensity. 'I could kill him! I'm not sure I won't strangle him with my bare hands!'

Watching her race towards the car park, Daniel doubted Ric was in any danger. He was not so sure about himself.

CHAPTER THIRTEEN

GLENNA scarcely registered the fact that Dr Simons' car was missing when she drew up outside his house. When Ric opened the door, his shirt half-unbuttoned as though he had still been dressing, she swept past him into the lounge and turned on him like an avenging angel.

'How *could* you!' she cried at him. 'How *dared* you!'

He eyed her flushed face and glittering eyes with wary speculation. She had not even stopped to pin up her hair.

'What am I supposed to have done now?'

'Not *now*! Eight years ago, you did it. Lied to me. Deceived me. Told me you didn't want me in your life. *Decided* for me that I couldn't take being married to a man who might become disabled. As though I was a little girl who had to have a happy ending for her fairy story.'

'Daniel,' he said quietly. 'I'll kill him,' he added, as Daniel had known that he would.

'No, I guessed. And I tricked Daniel into confirming my guess. What did they tell you might happen? Did Adrian know?'

'*No!*' He spoke sharply. 'They told me some time after the operation. When I was getting about a bit. I absolutely forbade them to tell anyone. It's a fifty-fifty chance, and if it does happen, they might try another 'operation, because then there would be nothing to lose.'

'And for a fifty-fifty chance—not even that, there's a possibility of a successful operation—you've wasted eight years, and were prepared to go on wasting the rest of our lives. Didn't it ever occur to you that I had a right to some say in my own future?'

He stood very still, his eyes narrow and unreadable. 'Aren't you rather jumping to conclusions?' he asked. 'As I reminded you once before, I've never said I loved you.'

'You never said you didn't, either,' Glenna answered swiftly.

She glared at him across the room, and stood taut and waiting. The silence stretched between them.

Ric moved, and turned to the sideboard that held a decanter of whisky and some glasses. She watched him pour some of the whisky into a glass. He was talking all the while.

'Look, Glenna,' he said. 'I got tired of these romantic games of yours eight years ago. I would have expected you to have grown out of them by now, too.' He tipped back his head and with his back still turned to her, drained the glass.

'It's very early in the morning to be drinking whisky,' she said severely, and he clutched the edge of the sideboard and bowed his head for a moment. She couldn't tell if that was anger or something else. An instant later he had turned to face her.

'It's an antidote to boredom,' he said.

'I am not *boring* you,' she said quite confidently. 'I never have. You're hoping it will give you some Dutch courage so that you can tell me to my face you've never loved me.'

'If I do, will you leave me?'

'Yes. I'll leave you alone and never ever bother you

again. I'll let you go out of my life and I won't even say goodbye. I'll live my life and you'll live yours, and we shall probably never meet again. And if I turn into a spinster schoolmarm in truth, or marry some man who will offer me a commitment to lifelong love, and accept mine, it will be none of your affair.' She stopped, looking at him defiantly. 'Tell me you don't love me, Ric.' She walked slowly towards him. 'Look at me,' she whispered, 'and tell me.'

'*Don't!*' he said harshly as she stopped two feet from him. His hands clutched at the sideboard behind him. Then they reached for her and she walked into his arms. 'I can't do it again,' he said, against her hair. 'It was bad enough the first time. I can't do it again.'

'You don't have to, my darling,' she said, tears finally washing away her anger with him.

'I love you,' he whispered, as though it was a guilty secret.

'I know, I know,' she assured him, in the gently shushing tone which one uses to a child needing comfort. 'I've always known.'

'I tried so hard to convince you that I didn't.'

'I know,' she said again. 'I'm sorry I made you be so cruel.'

'*You're* sorry! Oh, *sweet*!'

She smiled at his remorseful tone. 'It's your own fault if you feel guilty,' she told him. 'You've really been very stupid!'

'You sound as though you're dying to spank me!' He moved towards the sofa, taking her with him, and sat down with his arms still about her.

She chuckled. 'I told Daniel I'd strangle you with my bare hands.'

'Just you try!' Ric said warningly.

Glenna wasn't bothered, because he said it against

her lips, and the kiss that followed was anything but threatening.

Then suddenly he pushed her away and said, 'It doesn't make any difference, you know. I'm not going to tie you to a potential cripple.'

Fear made her voice sharp. Just when she thought she had won, here he was having scruples again. 'I really don't know why I bother with you!' she exclaimed. 'Your trouble is that you're already a cripple. You decided to be one eight years ago, and you've been behaving like one ever since!'

'What the hell does that mean?' he demanded. '*Decided?* There was no choice——'

'Yes, there was! Charlie said, when he found he was paralysed, he had two choices, to be a cripple, or to be a man who happened to be crippled. He decided to be a man. But you——!' she said with scorn, 'just because there was a chance you might be paralysed, you stopped living a normal life and started acting like a cripple.'

'I lead a perfectly normal life——'

'Do you? Most men of your age are married with families. When are you planning to get married?' Her eyes challenged him.

He sat looking at her for a long time, and her every muscle ached with tension.

'That depends,' he said at last, 'on whether a certain schoolteacher really wants to spend the rest of her life berating me, scolding me, telling me what a fool I am——'

'And loving you!' she said, falling into his ready arms. 'Am I really so shrewish?'

'Just schoolmarmish,' he grinned. 'I don't know how I kept my hands off you when you scolded me for drinking whisky so early in the morning.'

'Did you want to hit me so badly?'

'No, idiot!' he said. And showed her exactly what he

wanted to do.

'Do you realise,' he muttered against her cheek, a little later, 'that *you* never said you loved *me*, either?'

'I couldn't, because you didn't want me to,' she murmured. 'But you knew, anyway——' Suddenly she stiffened and drew back, staring at him. 'You did know, didn't you?'

'Oh, yes, I knew. If you knew how I longed, and dreaded, to hear you say it, my sweet, gallant darling.'

'I would have, if you'd asked me.'

'I couldn't do that. The one thing I was thankful for was that I hadn't told you when we were in France how I felt.'

Glenna stared at him accusingly. 'You knew *then*?'

'The very first time I kissed you. I knew then I wanted to marry you. But you were so young and inexperienced, and on holiday. It wouldn't have been fair to tie you then and there, although I was tempted. But I wouldn't have waited long, if it hadn't been for the damned accident.'

'Fool!' she said, but not as though she meant it. 'And you accused *me* of being self-sacrificing. I knew you didn't really want me to go away. I've never worn your bracelet.'

'I'll buy you a gold one to go with it—a wedding present. And you can give me that painting of yours.'

'Can I? Why?'

'That streak of gold—that ray of hope—reminds me of you.'

He raised his head as a car drew up outside. 'That'll be Dr Simons with Daniel.'

'He went to get Daniel? Of course, Daniel's car is still here, isn't it? I must have passed Dr Simons on my way here.' Glenna had been too angry to notice. 'We're going to tell them right away,' she said. 'Aren't we?'

'That you've proposed to me and I've accepted?' Ric gave a shout of laughter at the look on her face. 'I thought you'd forgotten how to blush!'

'Beast!' she laughed. 'I didn't!' Then, honesty getting the better of her, she added, 'Well, not in so many words.'

'Never mind,' he said soothingly. 'We'll just tell them we're getting married. Now?' he asked, as the two men, trying not to look intrigued, appeared in the doorway.

'Now.' Glenna declared firmly. 'Because once you've committed yourself in front of witnesses, you won't be able to bring yourself to jilt me. That noble streak of yours would never allow it!'

The Mills & Boon Rose is the Rose of Romance

Every month there are ten new titles to choose from — ten
new stories about people falling in love, people you want to
read about, people in exciting, far away places. Choose Mills
& Boon. It's your way of relaxing.

January's titles are:

BED OF GRASS by Janet Dailey
Judd Prescott had been the reason for Valerie leaving home.
Now she was back, but Judd still didn't know what that
reason had been . . .

WINTER WEDDING by Betty Neels
Professor Renier Jurres-Romeijn regarded Emily as a 'prim
miss'. So it wasn't surprising that he so obviously preferred her
lively sister Louise.

DANGEROUS DECEPTION by Lilian Peake
Anona Willis was engaged to the forceful Shane Brodie — but
he had admitted that he had no staying power where women
were concerned . . .

FEVER by Charlotte Lamb
The attraction between Sara Nichols and Nick Rawdon was
immediate — but somehow Sara could never clear up the
misunderstanding about her stepbrother Greg.

SWEET HARVEST by Kerry Allyne
Any thought of a reconciliation between herself and her
husband soon vanished when Alix realised that Kirby had
chosen her successor . . .

STAY THROUGH THE NIGHT by Flora Kidd
Virtually kidnapped aboard Burt Sharaton's yacht, Charlotte
was told that if she didn't co-operate with him, he would
ruin her father . . .

HELL OR HIGH WATER by Anne Mather
Jarret Manning was attractive, successful, experienced — and
Helen Chase felt mingled antagonism and fear every time she
met this disturbing man.

CANDLE IN THE WIND by Sally Wentworth
Shipwrecked, her memory lost, Sam had to believe her
companion Mike Scott when he told her she was his wife . . .

WHITE FIRE by Jan MacLean
Rana had fallen wildly in love with Heath Markland, to the
fury of her domineering mother. But perhaps she knew something about Heath that Rana didn't . . .

A STREAK OF GOLD by Daphne Clair
Eight years ago, Ric Burnett had cruelly told Glenna to get
out of his life — but now they had met again . . .

If you have difficulty in obtaining any of these books
from your local paperback retailer, write to:

Mills and Boon Reader Service
P.O. Box No 236, Thornton Road, Croydon, Surrey CR9 3RU